Witch in Winter

First published in Great Britain in 2019 by Simon & Schuster UK Ltd
A CBS COMPANY

Text Copyright © 2019 Kaye Umansky
Cover and interior illustrations Copyright © 2019 Ashley King

1 3 5 7 9 10 8 6 4 2

Simon & Schuster UK Ltd
1st Floor, 222 Gray's Inn Road
London
WC1X 8HB

www.simonandschuster.co.uk
www.simonandschuster.com.au
www.simonandschuster.co.in

Simon & Schuster Australia, Sydney
Simon & Schuster India, New Delhi

A CIP catalogue record for this book is available from the British Library.

PB ISBN: 978-1-4711-7562-6
eBook ISBN: 978-1-4711-7563-3

Printed and bound by CPI Group (UK) Ltd, Croydon, CR0 4YY

MIX
Paper from
responsible sources
FSC® C020471

KAYE UMANSKY

Witch in winter

Illustrated by
ASHLEY KING

To Andrew

PICKLES' RULES
OF CUSTOMER SERVICE

1. BE FRIENDLY
2. PRETEND THAT THE CUSTOMER IS ALWAYS RIGHT
3. BE A GOOD LISTENER
4. KEEP PEOPLE CHATTING
5. BE SYMPATHETIC
6. USE A SOOTHING TONE WITH THE TRICKY ONES
7. ALWAYS BE HELPFUL
8. STAY OPEN WHENEVER POSSIBLE
9. ALWAYS HAVE A STORE OF HANDY HANKIES
10. USE FLATTERY
11. DRAW ATTENTION TO A BARGAIN
12. NEVER SHOW SURPRISE
13. NEVER SHORT CHANGE
14. BE EFFICIENT
15. USE THE HARD SELL ONLY AS A LAST RESORT
16. ALWAYS HAVE CHANGE
17. DISPLAY THINGS NICELY
18. DO NOT GET INTO ARGUMENTS WITH CUSTOMERS
19. NEVER SHOUT
20. KEEP YOUR SENSE OF HUMOUR
21. APOLOGIZE FOR BAD WEATHER EVEN
THOUGH IT'S NOT YOUR FAULT
22. HANDLE ALL GOODS CAREFULLY
23. IF A CUSTOMER IS HOT, OFFER A COLD DRINK
24. DON'T TALK ABOUT TICKLE DUST
25. POLITENESS WORKS WONDERS

MAGENTA SHARP'S THREE RULES OF WITCHCRAFT

1. Read Instructions
2. Follow Recipe
3. Make It Work

SOME THINGS YOU NEED TO KNOW
BEFORE WE GET STARTED...

1. Elsie Pickles is training to be a witch. She didn't expect to. It just happened that way.

2. Elsie lives in the country town of Smallbridge, where she helps her dad out in the family shop, called Pickles' Emporium. The Pickles family live in the attic above the shop. They are: Elsie, her dad Albert, her mum Tilda, and her three little brothers – Arthy, Toby and baby Todd.

3. Life was pretty ordinary for Elsie until she met Magenta Sharp (known locally as the Red Witch, because she wears red from head to toe). Magenta lives in a magical moving tower which is usually based in Crookfinger Forest – the wild wood that borders Smallbridge – and after their first meeting Elsie agreed to tower-sit while Magenta was away. Elsie loved life at the tower and even grew to love its grumpy resident raven, Corbett – so she always jumps at the chance to visit Magenta and learn more about magic.

4. Elsie is now really good friends with two other residents of Crookfinger Forest: Joey the post boy

(who has a magical floating basket named Bill to help with his post round) and Sylphine Greenmantle (whose real name is Aggie Wiggins and always dresses like a wood sprite).

5. Elsie has a knack for magic. She can make it rain eggs – any kind – cooked or uncooked, including chocolate! She can conjure up small green frogs, which she sometimes dresses up, just for fun. She can brew a storm in a teacup. She can use a certain tone of voice to freeze people and creatures. She can even vanish in the blink of an eye and show up somewhere else! But she tries not to use magic too much because Smallbridge is an old-fashioned sort of

place and not that comfortable with new things.
(Although, a few months ago, the town was
besieged by witches, so it's not quite as stuffy as
it once was.)

But nothing much of interest has happened there
for a while now. A marrow competition. Weeks
of boring drizzle. A mislaid goat. Another week
of drizzle. The goat is found, safe and sound.
More drizzle. No, nothing exciting happens in
Smallbridge . . .

Until . . .

IT SNOWS!

Chapter One
SNOW

The snow began with a sudden blizzard that arrived in the night, sending the drizzle packing. It raced and raged from the frozen north, paused over Smallbridge and took an instant dislike to it. By the following morning, the whole town was snowed in. The river Dribble froze over. Huge, dangerous icicles hung from the lamp posts. The main street was waist-deep in white drifts. Towering banks of the stuff piled high against shop fronts and houses. Roofs groaned under the weight of it.

Smallbridge didn't know how to cope with snow. It didn't happen often enough for the town to plan for it. There was an old spade kept in the mayor's shed, together with a small toboggan and some bags of salt, none of which were any help at all, because as the snow fell, the shed was buried up to its roof.

The town dealt with the blizzard by doing nothing. It was a massive personal inconvenience that was best to ignore. Stay indoors, bank up the fire and live off the contents of cans dredged up from the backs of cupboards. When the thaw came, they would wait for Carl from the council to deal with the slush. Only then, when conditions were tolerable, would they venture out. Finally, the drama would pass into legend and life would return to normal.

But a week later, it was still snowing.

All was still strangely silent in Smallbridge. It should have been market day, which usually meant a busy and bustling town, but the only sounds were the faint whisper of falling flakes and the rush and plop of mini avalanches slithering down roofs. Even Nuisance, the town's stray dog, had abandoned his usual spot in the doorway of Pickles' Emporium and found somewhere warmer to sleep.

The snow lay so deep that the only way out of the houses was through upper windows using a ladder. That was much too adventurous for the people of Smallbridge. Why bother anyway? There was nowhere to go. They began to go stir-crazy. Losing their tempers and declaring that they hated their house, their granny and tinned kidney beans in prune juice.

And still it snowed.

Only Elsie Pickles didn't stay in. She went out.

★ ★ ★ ★

Elsie was getting rather good at witchcraft – although she kept it quiet because she didn't want to be gossiped about. Besides, her dad, Albert Pickles, liked her to concentrate on helping him in Pickles' Emporium, the family shop. It sold dull but useful things. String. Buckets. Ugly ornaments. Drawing pins.

Elsie quite liked working with her dad. He was very good at Customer Service and Elsie knew all the rules to follow to keep customers happy. (She found the rules came in handy for everyday life, too). But, oh dear, sometimes – well, a *lot* of the time – shopkeeping was *boring*.

But witchcraft? That's certainly not boring.

And neither is snow, so Elsie didn't want to miss it! Over the snowbound days, she went out quite often and didn't even need to climb through the bedroom window. Elsie knew how to take a short cut.

To witches, 'taking a short cut' means vanishing and popping up somewhere else. It's easy, actually. You just think the secret word (never say it out loud of course, it's secret), make a picture in your head of where you want to be and . . . there you are! Just like that. It doesn't hurt or even tickle.

Taking a short cut was particularly useful when your house was snowed in. Elsie wasn't enjoying being cooped up in the attic. Her mum and dad were worried about the shop being shut and losing money, so they sighed a lot. Arthy,

Toby and baby Todd were desperate to high-dive out of the window, which would *not* have been a good idea, so they weren't allowed, and that made them noisily sad or madly boisterous. The only time they stopped playing up was when they were asleep, listening to stories or eating jam.

At night, when the boys were asleep, Elsie would close the curtain between their bed and hers and do one of four things:

1. Go to bed because it was cold.
2. Sit at the window and watch snow falling in the dark.
3. Light a candle and quietly practise spells.
4. Take a short cut to the town library.

The last was her favourite. She would curl up in

the librarian's chair and read adventure stories by candlelight until her fingers were too cold to turn the pages. The deserted library was the only place of interest that Smallbridge could offer on a freezing night.

On the seventh night of snow, as the light began to fade, Elsie sat on the edge of her bed huddled up in shawls and decided to do a quiet bit of magic practice.

She had three solid little spells at her fingertips: the ones she learned on her first visit to

Magenta Sharp's magical tower. Eggs, frogs and storms in teacups. Elsie could conjure up lots of different eggs now – big, small, raw, cooked, brown, white – even chocolate! It was just a matter of various finger-waggles, usually combined with a short rhyme. Chocolate were the trickiest and made her thumbs ache.

Her frogs were getting fancier, too. She could do sweet little green ones, middle-sized brown ones and big, grinning, sploshy ones. If she really concentrated, she could produce a whole froggy dance team wearing top hats and carrying tiny canes!

On the other side of the curtain, her brothers were snoring. She lit the candle stub on the windowsill.

Right, thought Elsie. *Here goes. Easy stuff first.*

Wiggling her fingers and quietly mouthing the special words, she conjured up a small chocolate egg from the air, followed by a little green frog. This one wasn't wearing a top hat or carrying a cane; in fact, it looked a bit lost and cold. Elsie magicked it up a tiny woolly hat, gave it the chocolate egg and sent it back wherever it came from. She wondered about going to the kitchen and getting a teacup to make a storm in. Then she worried that the thunder might wake everyone else up . . . but maybe she would risk it? She needed to keep her hand in. That's what Magenta Sharp would say. Regular practice.

It had been a while since Elsie had seen Magenta. Through all those dreary weeks of drizzle and missing goats, Elsie had hoped the Red Witch would get in touch. Magenta's last business venture – a magic shop in Smallbridge, of all things – had come to a sudden, unexpected end (a long story, involving malfunctioning magical technology and some 'help' in the form of Sylphine Greenmantle, the worst shop assistant in the world). So now Magenta was settled back in Crookfinger Forest. She hadn't sent word for weeks and Elsie didn't quite have the courage to show up at the tower without an invitation.

Maybe being patient is all part of the witch training, thought Elsie. *I'll just keep practising.*

She waggled her fingers, which felt numb with the cold. How could she warm them up? Blowing on them never seemed to help. What would be really useful would be a warming spell. Was there such a thing? She couldn't remember one from any of the spell books she'd read. But there was nothing to say she couldn't make up one of her own . . . after all, she had the 'knack' for magic and warm was just a case of mixing hot and cold, right?

She looked at the candle on the windowsill. The flame provided heat, as well as light. There was her glass of water, so cold there were chips of ice in it. Hot and cold. Bind the two together with a little chant? Should work.

She reached out her left hand and carefully took hold of the candle. In her right hand, she lifted the clinking glass. Then she wiggled her chilly thumbs and whispered:

Hot and cold, cold and hot
Come together, hit the spot

The rhyme wasn't that good – but was it good enough?

The candle flame rose away from the wick and floated gracefully through the air across to the glass. It landed in the water and sank. The icy water gave a faint hiss and a brief gurgle, then settled down. Wisps of steam came from the glass.

Yes! thought Elsie happily. *I think I did it!*

She took the warm glass and wrapped her cold fingers around it, raised it to her lips and was just about to drink when she noticed something.

Outside, night was falling . . .

But the snow wasn't! The clouds were gone. The sky was speckled with stars and a huge, pale moon swam into view.

No more snow.

Chapter Two
A SURPRISE VISITOR

Elsie couldn't decide whether it was a good or a bad thing that the snow had stopped. It would be nice to be warm and eat fresh vegetables and to go for a walk and see people, but then what? Everything would go back to normal. And in no time, normal would become boring again.

At that point, suddenly, something came hurtling out of the night! It collided with the glass, making her jump back with a gasp. What was this horrible thing that had landed on her windowsill and was staring in at her with beady little eyes?

A harsh voice said: 'Jackdaws and giblets, let me in! It's perishing out here!'

'Corbett!' exclaimed Elsie, a delighted smile spreading across her face. 'It's you!'

'Who did you expect, Santa? Hurry up, I can't feel my claws.'

Elsie opened the window with difficulty. Snow had built up on the sill. A small avalanche slithered over the ledge as it jerked open. Corbett hopped inside, furiously shaking off white flakes. Cold air filled the room, and Elsie hastily pulled the window shut.

'That,' he announced, 'was horrible!'

'*Sssh*, keep your voice down, the boys are asleep.' Elsie patted the bed beside her. 'Come and sit down. Here's my shawl, make yourself a little nest. Shall I dry you off a bit? I've just made a hot drink, do you want some? Oh, it's *so* good to see you!'

'Stop fussing, I'm fine. Look, I'm not stopping. There's no one at the tower!'

'Why? Where's Magenta?'

'Gone. That's why I'm here.'

'What? How? Why? When?'

'The day before the blizzard. She didn't come down for breakfast. I thought she was sulking in her room.'

'Had you two had an argument?' asked Elsie. Magenta and Corbett's relationship involved a lot of bickering. They both seemed to enjoy it.

'Well, yes,' confessed Corbett. 'The night before she was complaining about my supper. Said it put her off hers.'

'What was your supper?'

'Worms.'

'I expect hers was spaghetti, was it?'

'How did you know?' Corbett sounded astonished.

'Just a guess. Was that all? A silly argument about food?'

'Yes. But it got a bit heated. We were both a bit . . . mean to each other and in the end Magenta said I was the world's worst bird to live with and stomped off to bed. I thought she was just being petty, but then she didn't come down at all the next day, so I checked on her. I had terrible problems opening the bedroom door – big round knob, you know – nearly dislocated my beak. Finally got in, bed not slept in, no note, nothing.'

'Has she done it before?' asked Elsie. 'Vanished in the night?'

'Occasionally. But she always tells me or leaves a note. It's one of the tower's rules: *When off you go, the bird shall know.* It means the resident raven has to be informed of the witch's whereabouts.' Corbett shook his glossy head. 'Something's not right, Elsie. I wanted to come and get you before but I had to wait for the snow to stop. I'm taking a risk being here now because I'm not supposed to go very far. That's another tower rule.'

'I remember it,' said Elsie. *'Bad Luck Will Come to Stay Should the Raven Fly Away.'*

'That's the one. I've got to get back. I'm worried the tower will go looking for a new owner.'

'It won't,' said Elsie. She paused. 'Will it?'

'It could,' said Corbett. 'It's a working tower, built for a single purpose – to provide a perfect home for anyone of a *magical* nature – usually a witch, although it doesn't have to be. A raven always comes with it, all part of the package. If the witch and the raven are both away, it starts giving off sort of – empty vibes. *I've been deserted! Why don't you come and live in me?* That sort of thing. *Anyone* could just walk in. A *bad* person could take it! And we'll never see it again.'

'I see. So that's why Magenta wanted me to house-sit that first time. Although I wasn't a witch then.'

'Yes, you were. You just didn't know it. Anyway, Elsie, we need to find Magenta. What if something bad has happened to her?'

His voice cracked and he wiped his eyes with a wing. Elsie had never seen him like this. Customer Service Rule Five clicked in. Sympathy was clearly called for.

'Hey,' she said, poking him playfully on his feathery chest. 'Stop that. What are you thinking the worst for? There's probably a perfectly good explanation. I'll come right away. I'll just write a quick note to Mum and Dad and pack a few things, in case I need to stay a while. We'll collect Nuisance on the way.'

'Thanks.' Corbett gave a little shiver. 'Never thought I'd say it, but I miss her. It's lonely on my own with the snow all around. No one's come calling. Not even the Howler sisters.'

'What about the post?' asked Elsie. 'Has Joey called in?'

'No,' said Corbett. 'A carrier pigeon told me all postal deliveries have stopped until conditions improve. Come on, Elsie, let's go. Let's go *now*.'

Nuisance's ears pricked up at the snowy crunch of approaching footsteps. He had been curled up beneath a pile of old sacks in the bottom of the broken wheelbarrow he called home ever since the snow started. It wasn't a bad choice. The sacks were smelly and scratched a bit – but then again, Nuisance was smelly and scratched a bit. At least they were warm, and the thick layer of snow on top provided good insulation.

Conveniently, it was just along the alley from the Emporium, where Elsie lived. Kind, clever Elsie, who told him he was a good dog, brought him sausages and took him on exciting adventures.

'Nuisance?' came a voice. 'Are you in there?'

Yippee! It was Elsie!

Funny. She didn't usually arrive at night. Still . . .

Nuisance poked his head out into the freezing air. His ears were pricked and his eyes were bright.

Oh-ho. Perched on Elsie's shoulder was that grouchy Corbett bird from the tower in the woods. That could only mean an adventure was about to happen!

And look at that! The snow had stopped falling. That was new. And a big, yellow moon and stars! All new! Wow! What a great world!

'Greetings, dog,' said Corbett. 'It's been a while.'

Nuisance thumped his tail happily.

'No sausages,' said Elsie. 'Sorry.'

Oh. His tail drooped. No sausages.

'I promise I'll get you some as soon as we get to the tower. Magenta's gone missing and we have to find her. You want to come along, don't you, boy?'

Yes! Oh yes! He wanted to come all right. This was the best thing that had happened since – well, since the last time. He wiggled out from under the sacks, jumped into Elsie's arms and licked her chin.

'Steady on!' snapped Corbett, from Elsie's shoulder. 'You're in my parking space.'

'Okay, both of you, keep still,' said Elsie. 'I need to concentrate. We're taking a short cut.'

And all three of them disappeared. Just like that.

Chapter Three
THE TOWER

Deep in Crookfinger Forest, the tower stood on the edge of a snow-filled glade, pointing up like a finger through the surrounding trees. All the shutters were closed. The red flag was frozen at half-mast. The doorstep was buried deep in snow. It looked lonely in the moonlight. Lonely and . . . unhappy.

And suddenly, there they were! Elsie, Nuisance and Corbett. Standing before the doorstep, their breath making little puffs in the freezing air.

'You see, Corbett?' said Elsie. 'I knew it wouldn't go off without you— hey! What's up with *you*?'

Nuisance was scrabbling in her arms, desperate to be let down. At the same time, there came a sudden rustling noise from the far side of the tower, which lay deep in shadow. Followed by the crunching sound of . . . *running footsteps*!

Nuisance let out a shrill bark, leapt from Elsie's arms and went bouncing across the snow in a series of stiff-legged little leaps before being swallowed by the shadows.

'What was all that about?' said Elsie as Nuisance's barking receded into the distance.

'Who knows?' said Corbett. 'Maybe the Howlers saw the place empty and came snooping around hoping to steal something. Or maybe someone's already scoping it out. To see if it's up for grabs.'

Maybe, thought Elsie. The last suggestion seemed unlikely. But it could be the Howler Sisters. She knew Nuisance really didn't like them. Evie and Ada, two little old ladies with sweet smiles and parasols – and wolf tails – who were extremely light fingered and had a thing about buckets. On the other hand, there were two of them and it had sounded like just the one lot of footsteps.

'Is the front door locked?' she asked Corbett.

'Of course,' said Corbett. 'I'll fly down the chimney and get the key.'

'Wait one second.' Elsie crunched to the doorstep and looked up. 'Hello, Tower,' she said. 'Can I come in, please?'

Instantly, with no hesitation whatsoever, the

front door swung open.

In the tiny hallway, a lamp hanging on a hook glowed into life, all by itself. Elsie stepped in and Corbett flew in behind her just as the door gently closed. The floor and walls vibrated as the tower gave what felt like a little shiver of welcome combined with . . . what? Relief? Was that it? Anyway, Elsie knew it was pleased to see her.

★ ★ ★ ★

A short time later, a cheerful fire was crackling up the chimney, the curtains were drawn and all the lamps were alight. Elsie was curled up in the rocking chair with a mug of hot cocoa and a large slice of banana cake provided by the tower's magic larder. It was good to eat something other than tinned soup and endless eggs. She happily wiggled her toes in the heat. Corbett sat on his wooden perch in the corner, looking droopy.

Idly, Elsie conjured up a little thunderstorm in her cocoa mug. In between sips, waves rippled across the brown surface, as though blown by a tiny wind. Every so often, a tiny bolt of lightning would shoot down from the miniature cloud that hovered just above the rim, followed by a little roll of thunder. As a drink, it was both comforting *and* interesting.

'We need to make a plan,' said Elsie. 'First, are you absolutely sure Magenta didn't leave a note? You looked in her office?'

'Of course. Bedroom, office, privy door, teapot, everywhere. Nothing.'

'When it's light, we'll try the Spelloscope,'

said Elsie.

The Spelloscope lived at the very top of the tower. It was a long brass tube mounted on a tripod. You pressed the special magic button on the side, said the name of whoever it was you were looking for and you'd be able to see them, wherever they were, at the end of the tube! You could zoom in, zoom out, even hear them talking.

'It's not working,' said Corbett. 'The glass has cracked with the frost and the magic button's frozen.'

'We could try looking in the *Everything You Need To Know* book,' suggested Elsie. The book had been left by Magenta the first time Elsie tower-sat and had proved very helpful. It really *did* seem to know everything you'd need to know.

'The only thing we need to know is where Magenta *put* it. You know the state she lets the drawers get in.'

Corbett opened his beak in a huge yawn. 'Sorry, Elsie. I haven't been sleeping well. Can we do this in the morning? I'm too tired to think straight.'

'Of course,' said Elsie, yawning as she suddenly realized how tired she was too. 'I'm ready for bed as well. I'll just see if Nuisance is back.'

He wasn't. The moon picked out the paw prints in the snow, leading away into the dark trees. Elsie fetched the broom and swept the doorstep clear of snow, then she made Nuisance up a little bed on the step, using the kitchen mat and the rug from the rocking chair. It was bitterly cold. He would be glad of something to snuggle into when he returned. Unasked, the tower thoughtfully conjured up two sausages from the magic larder. Elsie left them outside with a bowl of water.

She locked the door and made sure the shutters on the kitchen window were properly bolted. She cleaned her teeth, put the fire guard in place and turned out the lamps, leaving just one candle alight.

'Good night, Corbett,' she called softly into the dark corner. No answer. Just an exhausted snore.

Elsie took the candle and climbed the stairs to the little blue room that she had come to think of as hers. It was too dim to see much, but she could see the picture of the Emporium that hung over the bed. The image always seemed to change each time she visited. This time, the shop was covered in snow.

She had a feeling there would be new clothes waiting for her in the wardrobe – the tower seemed to enjoy spoiling her in that way – but she would wait to find out in the morning. Because that wonderful bed waited. The bed that was like floating on the softest clouds. The bed that provided the best sleep ever.

★ ★ ★ ★

In a faraway part of the forest, Nuisance stood panting by a holly bush. He had really enjoyed the chase. It had been great! Running through a snowy forest at night was much more exciting than sitting in the middle of Smallbridge main street with his begging paw dangling, which is what he did most of the year. Chasing was dog-like! It brought a shine to the eyes, a woof to the lips and a jaunty wag to the tail!

Sadly, it was over now. Rather to his surprise, whatever or *whoever* he had been chasing had vanished. The running footsteps had suddenly cut off. Silence. Nothing. Gone.

Nuisance stood and listened for a moment or two. He ran on a few paces so that he could tell himself he'd done a thorough job, then stopped because there was clearly no point. He might as well go back to the tower. Hopefully there would be a sausage waiting. Besides, it was getting colder. *Much* colder. So cold, that his nose was actually hurting. It felt as though tiny, invisible teeth were nipping it.

And then . . .

Nuisance's ears pricked up. He heard the sound of jangling bells.

Now, *jingling* bells are lovely – high and silvery, gentle on the ear. But *jangling* bells are different. They sound harsh and tinny, like saucepans bashing together. They set your teeth on edge and make you desperately wish that they would stop.

And now these horrible, head-hurting, cracked, jangling bells were coming closer. And what were those other sounds? Crunching hooves, heavy breathing and a sort of weird, whooshy, slithering noise . . .

Nuisance dropped onto his belly and backed bottom-first into the holly bush. Whatever was coming, he didn't like the sound of it. He would hide in this bush and he wouldn't move a whisker until it had gone.

Oh my! Here it was . . .

Through the trees came . . . what? Nuisance didn't know. He had never seen anything like it!

He knew what it *wasn't*. It wasn't a wagon or a cart or

a coach, because it didn't have wheels. Nuisance knew about wheels. Back in Smallbridge, he sometimes lay on his back in the middle of the road, rolling in the dirt and causing the traffic to back up. It was doing things like that that got him his name. But this – this *thing* was wheel-less.

Instead, it had runners. Sleek, extra-extra-long silver runners that reared up at the front, like a curling wave. The runners made it into a sleigh. But this sleigh was quite unusual. Because instead of a seat or bench on top of the runners, there was an entire house!

The house appeared to be carved entirely from ice. It had four windows and a door. Jagged icicles hung from the roof, like serrated teeth. The windows were coated with thick, black ice, so you couldn't see inside. Whoever lived there clearly didn't go in for flowery curtains and colourful window boxes.

The sleigh-house was pulled by – well, what else? A huge reindeer! But it wasn't the happiest-looking of creatures. It had angry yellow teeth, angry little eyes and two enormous sets of angry antlers growing out of its broad forehead. The jangling bells hung on a chain around its neck and the reindeer was clearly not pleased about this arrangement. At a glance you could tell that any mention of toys, Santa or happy little children around *this* reindeer would be a bad idea.

Nuisance, staring at this extraordinary apparition from the shelter of the holly bush, could make no sense of it. Bad bells. Big, angry animal with a twig hairdo. Weird iced house on skis. Overall air of menace. (Stray dogs are

good at spotting menace.)

A sharp command came from inside the sleigh house.

'*Spike! 'Old up.*'

The reindeer stopped. So, thankfully, did the jangling.

The voice spoke again and this time three other voices joined in:

''Ow much furver?' demanded the first voice impatiently.

'Ain't sure,' replied a second. 'Still a way, I fink.'

'You found the tower, you saw the tower, and now you ain't sure where the blinkin' tower is. That's what you're tellin' me?'

'It's confusin' out there, Dad,' whined the second. 'All the trees look the same in the dark. An' I 'ad a mad dog on me heels, din' I?'

'You shoulda frosted it!' snapped voice one. 'What do I keep tellin' you? You got the power, use it!'

Voice two mumbled indistinctly.

'What?' said voice one. 'What are you sayin'?'

'Ma says we're not to,' mumbled voice two.

'Well, yer ma's not here, is she? Right now you're with me, an' we do fings my way, right?'

There came more indistinct mumbling from voice two.

'So you're tellin' me,' sneered voice one, 'that a little doggy barked at you and now you can't find the way back.'

'I ain't got a map in me 'ead, 'ave I?' protested voice two.

'You got nothin' in your head, son. Shoulda sent yer brother to look.'

'Like he'd do better,' said voice two sulkily.

'I would too!' said a new, third voice.

'I'm fed up of goin' round in circles,' broke in a fourth voice, female this time. 'I wanna go to bed.'

'So you shall, princess, so you shall,' said the first voice, sweetly doting this time. 'Spike!' it shouted. 'I'm callin' it off for tonight! Find us a campsite.'

Nuisance watched as Spike the reindeer moved angrily off, evil bells jangling, hauling the strange house away through the trees.

What did it all mean?

Nuisance didn't know. He was a dog.

He should tell Elsie. She'd know what was going on.

If only he could talk.

Chapter Four
JOEY

The following morning, when Elsie went down to the kitchen, a welcome surprise greeted her.

'Good night's sleep?' said a voice through a mouthful of crunchy toast.

'Joey!' Elsie was delighted to see her friend. Sometimes, Joey had good ideas. And no matter what, he was always cheerful, meaning you couldn't help being cheerful, too. Corbett was sitting on the chair back and looked like he was already in a better mood.

'I know where Her Witchiness keeps the spare key,' said Joey. 'I let myself in, banked up the fire and ordered myself some breakfast. Hope you don't mind.'

''Course not,' said Elsie, going to the magic larder. Usually she liked to make her own breakfast, but today there were important things to do so magic would be quicker. 'I'm so pleased you're here.'

'I've given Nuisance a breakfast sausage.'

'Ah. He's back then,' said Elsie, relieved. 'He ran off as soon as we got here last night. Chasing off an intruder.'

'The Howler sisters, we think,' said Corbett. 'I must say I'm impressed you made it through the snow, Joey. Quite the hero.'

'That's me,' agreed Joey.

Elsie knocked three times on the larder door. 'Can I have toast and honey, please, Tower? And a glass of apple juice.'

'It's bitterly cold outside,' said Joey. 'I brought Bill inside to warm up. Don't want him going rusty.'

Elsie looked over at the wire shopping basket that was currently sitting directly in front of the fire, hogging the heat and vibrating happily like a purring cat. Since they met at the Sorcerer's Bazaar, Joey and Bill had been inseparable. Their relationship was a cross between a pet and a friend. Rather handily, Bill floated, so he was very useful on Joey's post round.

'Still working out, then?' asked Elsie. 'Bill?'

'I'll say. He's perfect. Right, mate?' He reached over and gave the basket an affectionate pat.

'Has Corbett told you Magenta's gone missing?' asked Elsie. The larder door swung open, displaying Elsie's breakfast order. 'Thanks, Tower.'

'Of course I did,' said Corbett. 'The second he arrived.'

'I don't suppose you've heard anything, Joey?'

'Well, no. But then, I haven't talked to anyone apart from my mum since the snow came. Can't do my round, too dangerous, health and safety and all that. I'm here on my own time. I came to check everyone's okay, like the hero Corbett says I am.'

'Have you been to see Sylphine?'

'Not yet. She comes next on my heroic visiting list. Any ideas what to do about Her Witchiness?'

'Well, for a start, the Spelloscope's out. Corbett says it's broken.'

'You can forget the copy of *Everything You Need To Know* too. I've looked. Nowhere to be found,' Corbett told her.

'I could try looking through the spell books in the office?' said Elsie. 'Perhaps I can find a recipe for some sort of – I don't know – tracking spell.'

'You could,' said Joey. 'But wouldn't it make more sense to ask her best friend?'

'What best friend?'

'Wendy Snipe.'

'I wouldn't call Wendy her best friend,' said Elsie. 'Magenta doesn't even like her much.'

'So? Her Witchiness doesn't like anybody much, and besides, Wendy and her friends know all the gossip going round.'

Elsie had met Wendy Snipe (the Wise Woman of Clackham Common) and her two friends, Maureen (the Hag of Heaving Heath) and Madame Shirley (Fortune Teller To The Stars) a few times now, and Joey was right. If anyone knew where Magenta was, they would.

'You're right,' she agreed. 'But I can't take a short cut like I did from Smallbridge to here, because I've never been to Wendy's cottage, so I can't picture it in my head.'

'We can go the old-fashioned way and walk together,' said Joey. 'I know where she lives because I deliver her post, remember? She runs a wise woman business, and gets all these cards saying *Thanks For Your Great Wisdom*.' He gave a little chuckle. 'I think she sends them to herself because they're all in the same handwriting.'

'Thanks,' said Elsie gratefully. 'I was hoping you'd come.'

'We should top up on toast now because we won't get anything nice to eat when we get there,' went on Joey. 'I've been delivering to her for ever and never even been offered a cup of tea. She always claims she's out of milk. What about you, Corbs? You coming?'

'I'll stay here,' said Corbett. 'I shouldn't leave the tower alone and someone needs to be in if . . . *when* Magenta gets back. Be as quick as you can, though, Elsie. The tower shouldn't be without a witch for too long.'

Chapter Five
SYLPHINE

Sylphine Greenmantle – real name Aggie Wiggins – wasn't crazy about snow. She didn't have the right sort of clothes, as her wardrobe was more suited to dancing barefoot under the moon on summer nights. Sylphine had an image of herself as some magical fairy creature. She favoured long, wafty dresses and floaty scarves, mostly in green, because green was what wood sprites wore. And she had masses of wild, free-flowing hair, which she liked to put flowers in. It was wasted under a woolly hat.

The snow had made a lot of work for Sylphine, too. She was mad about animals and her garden was filled with scratching posts and ponds and food trays and encouraging little notices of welcome to entice the local wildlife. Mostly, animals tried to avoid Sylphine's cottage for fear of being caught and hugged into submission. But since the snow, every hungry creature had been turning up and eating all the food she put out. This was good, because her garden was stuffed with animal visitors, but bad because she spent all her time wrestling sacks of pellets and bales of straw up from the cellar, while wearing ugly, clumpy work boots teamed with an awful warm brown coat given to her by her grandma.

Seven days of snow was enough. Sylphine

was fed up with it now. Plus, there was an emergency: she was out of shampoo. Sylphine used a special magical anti-frizz shampoo that Magenta Sharp made for her. It was expensive, but it did what it said on the bottle:

MAKES HAIR LONGER AND SHINIER THAN OTHER SHAMPOOS. BUY IT OR BE SORRY.

Running out of shampoo was almost as bad as running out of food, so she decided there was nothing for it but to wrap up warm and walk to the tower for a new supply. That was assuming the tower was there, of course. Sometimes it moved to different locations within the forest, and occasionally it visited other dimensions entirely.

Sylphine put on three wafty dresses on top of each other and reached in the wardrobe for the awful brown coat. Then she shook her head and put it back again. Instead, she hacked a hole in a blanket with a pair of scissors, stuck her head through, added several scarves and shawls, pulled a shapeless woolly hat over her unwashed hair, pulled on extra socks, and finally pushed her moon-dancing feet into the clumpy work boots.

Sylphine examined herself in the hall mirror, gave a little sigh and hoped she wouldn't bump into anyone. At least she wasn't wearing the coat.

★ ★ ★ ★

Elsewhere in the forest, another expedition was

on its way. Elsie, Joey, Nuisance and Bill were crunching their way through the snow – and Elsie was loving it! Snow was so much better in the woods than it was in Smallbridge. The forest looked beautiful, like it had been carved from a wedding cake. Better still, she had her friends with her. And it was nice to have a proper walk for the first time in over a week. Even though worrying about Magenta made them all quieter than usual.

Every so often, one of them would lob a sneaky snowball. Once, they stopped in a glade for a short but giggly snowball fight. Nuisance ran round barking madly, then went racing off with Bill to play hide and seek among the trees.

But the fun didn't last long, because there wasn't time. The Red Witch was missing. This was serious stuff.

They moved deeper into the forest, Joey leading the way. The snow was dangerously deep in places, and at times they had to duck under branches so heavily laden that they seemed on the point of cracking, but Joey seemed to know exactly the right route to take.

Elsie had looked into the wardrobe before setting out, and sure enough, the tower had come up trumps yet again – this time providing a warm winter coat in blue, her favourite colour, plus a matching hat and a pair of huge, fluffy mittens. Despite her new clothes, the air took her breath away. Joey didn't seem to feel the cold so much, but then he was used to being out in all weathers. So was Nuisance, who showed no signs of flagging. Bill sailed easily around the tree trunks.

I really must stop taking short cuts, thought

Elsie. *This walk is making me puff.*

'How much further?' she asked. It seemed to be getting even colder. Her feet and hands had gone numb. The end of her nose was actually beginning to hurt.

'Not far now,' said Joey. 'Left at the big oak, then sharp right and it's just ahead. There's a big sign in the front garden that says:

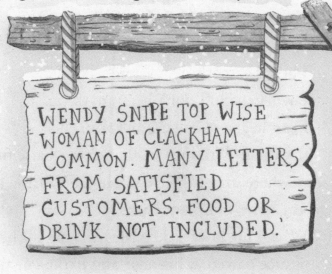

WENDY SNIPE TOP WISE WOMAN OF CLACKHAM COMMON. MANY LETTERS FROM SATISFIED CUSTOMERS. FOOD OR DRINK NOT INCLUDED.'

'If she's the Wise Woman of Clackham Common, what's she doing living in Crookfinger Forest?' asked Elsie. 'Ouch,' she added. 'The tip of my nose is really *hurting*.'

'She said the Common was too draughty, and she can't be bothered to change the sign.' Joey rubbed the end of his nose. '*Ow*. So is mine. *Ow, ouch*!'

Elsie suddenly grabbed his arm.

'What?'

'I heard something. Listen.'

Joey listened. 'I don't hear anything.'

'I can hear . . . bells. Can't you?'

Just then, Nuisance came bolting back from somewhere under the trees. He ran to Elsie and gave a series of urgent barks.

'What's up, boy?' said Elsie, ruffling his head. Nuisance pawed at his nose and barked again.

Seconds later, Bill came zooming up, landed with a thump in Joey's arms and tried to snuggle in. This was very unbasketty behaviour.

'What's up with them?' said Joey.

'I don't know,' said Elsie. She gave a frown. 'But I know I heard bells. This is weird. Let's hurry up. I'm *freezing*.'

Sylphine wasn't enjoying walking through the snowy forest. The trailing scarves were turning out to be a problem, because she kept treading on the ends and falling over. A low branch had hooked off her hat. Also, she was more than ready for lunch. Something hot from the tower's magic larder – a mug of chocolate and a slice of ginger cake, perhaps. Or a bowl of soup and a plate of toast. Crumpets. Anything. Witch Sharp didn't exactly welcome visitors, but even she wouldn't leave someone standing outside in the cold. Would she?

Actually, thought Sylphine, *she might.*

Sylphine had steered clear of Magenta since an unfortunate incident in Smallbridge involving her newly opened magic shop. Not only had Sylphine accidentally put the shop out of business, she had put it out of *existence*. Long story, most of it bad. Luckily, Magenta had been getting bored with shopkeeping anyway, but it hadn't been the best way for her to end her retail career.

To Sylphine's relief, when she arrived in the clearing, the tower was in its usual place. She was just about to cross the glade when a familiar voice spoke just above her head:

'She's not here.'

Corbett was hunched on a low branch, staring down with his black, beady eyes. His feathers were fluffed against the cold.

'Oh,' said Sylphine. 'Hello, Corbett. How are you?'

'I've been better.'

From a nearby tree, a robin suddenly struck up a happy song.

'Push off, twig legs!' shouted Corbett. 'May your daft red breast turn out to be a rash.'

The robin said something sharp in Bird.

'Fly over here and say that,' snarled Corbett.

The robin decided not to push its luck and flew away.

'Are you moulting again?' asked Sylphine. 'You're very snappy.'

'No. Magenta's missing.'

'Oh my. How come?'

'How do I know? No note, just gone. And it might just be my fault.'

'Why?'

'We had an argument about worms. She said they put her off her supper.'

'Spaghetti, I expect,' nodded Sylphine.

'How did you—? Anyway, I haven't seen her since. The tower's been without a witch, so I fetched Elsie. She and the dog have gone off to see Wendy Snipe. With Joey and the basket.'

'Oh. Without me?' Sylphine felt a little miffed.

'They were in a hurry.'

'Where does Wendy Snipe live?'

'A mile or so as the raven flies.'

'Is that the same as the crow flies?'

'Yes, but better.'

Sylphine thought about this. A mile or so. That was a long way. On the other hand, it was a long way home without lunch and her hair desperately needed a wash. Magenta might not be here but hopefully she would have a stash of the special shampoo in a cupboard somewhere. *Failing that*, Sylphine thought, *I'll ask Elsie to magic me some up.*

'How long do you think they'll be?' she asked.

'Haven't a clue. You can't come in and wait. The door's locked. Besides, I'm not in the mood for company. If you want to find 'em, follow the footprints.' He pointed a claw at the mixture of human and doggy footprints that led away through the trees. 'Or don't. I don't care either way.'

'Cheer up, Corbett,' said Sylphine.

'I don't think it's your fault that Witch Sharp's missing. A silly little row about worms isn't enough to make someone disappear. It has to be something much more serious. Kidnapped by goblins, maybe, or lost at sea, perhaps an accident or something. Maybe she's fallen down a cave and lost her memory so she can't magic herself out.'

'Thanks for that,' said Corbett bleakly. 'Thanks a lot.'

'You're welcome,' said Sylphine. 'Happy to be of service.'

Corbett took off and flapped up to the top of the tower, where he perched on the broken Spelloscope and stared off into the distance, hoping in vain to see a flash of red.

Chapter Six
THREE WITCHES

'Biscuit?' asked Wendy Snipe.

'No, thank you,' chorused Elsie and Joey.

They were squeezed on to a too-small sofa in the cluttered living room. Wendy Snipe went in for knick-knacks. The surface of every sideboard and spindly table was covered with tiny pots and fiddly little ornaments that Nuisance would have instantly knocked to the floor if he had come in. Being strictly an outside dog, he hadn't. He and Bill had elected to squeeze into the tiny porch, alongside a mop, a dead spider plant and a collection of broomsticks. They both seemed a little spooked.

'Well, if nobody wants it, I'll put it away.' Wendy reached over and picked up the tin of biscuits. Or rather, the tin of a biscuit. There was only the one. It looked small, dry and unappetising.

'I wouldn't say no to a cup of tea, though,'

added Joey. He gave Elsie a private little nudge.

'Not sure if I've got any milk,' Wendy said. 'I'll check.'

She bustled out into the kitchen, taking the tin of a biscuit with her.

'Wise decision,' said a mournful voice from the armchair in a corner. 'She's offered that biscuit to everyone for the last six months.'

The voice belonged to Maureen, the Hag of Heaving Heath. She was long and thin and favoured the traditional witchy clothing of black cloak and tall, pointy hat, which currently sat beside her on the floor.

'The last biscuit's always the worst,' observed a second voice from the opposite corner. 'I wouldn't hold out much hope for that milk either.'

This was Madame Shirley, Fortune Teller

to the Stars. In contrast to Maureen, Shirley was a riot in a paint shop. Orange turban and turquoise dress. Pink high-heeled shoes. Gold bangles. Scarlet lipstick. Bright green eyeshadow. It hurt the eyes to look at her. The large, yellow china teapot she used for her fortune telling sat by her feet.

Both of them had already been at Wendy's when Elsie and Joey were ushered inside, stamping the snow off their boots. Elsie had the feeling that these three particular witches spent a lot of time in each other's houses.

'Wendy's not known for her hospitality,' Maureen told Elsie and Joey. 'She might have the whole cosy-motherly-favourite-aunty-kind-granny vibe, but she's definitely missing the feeding-people-up urge.'

'Her wisdom's good, though, to be fair,' said Shirley.

'Oh, yes,' agreed Maureen. 'I'm not saying she's not wise. Just mean.'

Wendy Snipe came bustling back.

'Sorry, loves, all out of milk,' she told them sadly. 'So,' she beamed around. 'What are we all talking about?'

'You,' said Maureen. 'And how mean you are.'

'I don't call it *mean*, Maureen. I call it being careful.'

'Admit it, dear, you're tight with the catering,' said Shirley. 'You're not like those old-fashioned witches who used to stay up all night making gingerbread to fatten up children. Sorry for mentioning that,' she added to Elsie and Joey.

'No problem,' chorused Elsie and Joey politely.

'Anyway,' said Shirley. 'If you're not feeding these kids, Wendy, let's at least find out what it is they want. I don't s'pose this is just a social visit.'

'You're right!' cried Wendy. 'Madge send you for supplies, did she, Elsie dear? What's she run out of this time?'

'No,' said Elsie. 'Magenta's actually gone missing. We were wondering if you've heard anything.'

'She's been gone a week,' said Joey. 'No note. She didn't say anything to Corbett, like he says she's supposed to.'

'You don't want to take any notice of that *gloomy* bird,' said Maureen. 'That *crow*. It's always moaning and going on about rules. That's the disadvantage of living in a magical moving tower. You have to put up with the crow that comes with it.'

'He's a raven,' Joey corrected, adding, 'you're right, though, he does like a moan.'

'We haven't seen anything of Madge anyway,' said Shirley. 'Not since the vanishing shop affair.'

'Shame,' chorused Wendy and Maureen although you could tell they didn't really mean it.

'We hoped you could help us find her,' said Elsie.

'I'll try and raise her on the ball if you like.' said Wendy.

She pulled open a sideboard drawer. Politely, everyone looked away. What's in a witch's private cupboards and drawers is secret. And almost always incredibly untidy.

Wendy rummaged around and finally emerged with a large, grubby-looking crystal ball. As well as greasy fingerprints, it had a bad crack. 'Here we are. Could do with a bit of a polish. Never mind, it'll do.'

She swiped the ball on her sleeve, waved a hand over it and said:

'Wendy Snipe calling Magenta Sharp. Madge? You there? Come in, will you?'

The ball just sat there, looking dirty.

'Come on, Madge,' said Wendy. 'Show yourself. I've got young Elsie here. She just wants a quick word.'

Nothing.

'I'll try reading the tea leaves,' said Shirley. 'I always bring my own, I know I won't get any here.' She picked up the teapot and headed for the kitchen.

Chapter Seven
COLD MAGIC

Shirley came tottering back in on her pink high heels. In her hands was a tray bearing the yellow teapot, a small china cup and saucer and a long spoon.

'Right,' she said, depositing the tray on the table. 'I'll just give it a stir.'

Steam puffed up as she removed the pot lid and stirred the contents three times with the spoon. Then she replaced the lid, picked up the pot and poured tea into the cup.

'Have to let the leaves settle,' she said. 'Talk

amongst yourselves.'

'So,' Wendy turned to the children. 'You walked all the way from the tower. How was the journey?'

'Fun,' chorused Joey and Elsie.

'Until right at the end when it got absolutely freezing.' Elsie added.

'Around the time you thought you heard the bells,' Joey said to her.

Wendy and Maureen exchanged a startled glance.

'Did they jingle or jangle?' asked Maureen. 'The bells?'

'Jangled,' said Elsie. 'Even in the distance, they sounded horrible.'

'And then it got colder, you say?' said Wendy.

'Freezing,' said Elsie. 'It made our noses hurt. Why?'

Maureen and Wendy exchanged another look. They were about to speak when Shirley clapped her hands, sat up straight and beamed around.

'That's nice and ready now!' she said and picked up the cup, curled her hands around it and peered into its depths. She frowned. 'Oh. Well, well. There's a thing.'

'What?' chorused everyone.

'I've been hacked.' Slowly, Shirley turned the cup upside down. A solid lump of brownish ice dropped out, fell to the floor and skidded off under a small side table.

'What?' said Elsie. 'What does that mean?'

'It means there's cold, strong magic at work,' said Shirley. 'Outside interference.'

'You know who's behind this, don't you? There are enough clues,' said Wendy.

Maureen nodded. 'Snow that never thaws, jangling bells, nipped noses, cold hacking. All points to one thing.'

'What?' cried Elsie, feeling very confused. 'What does it all point to?'

Heavily, in a doleful chorus, the three witches said two words:

'Jack Frost.'

'You don't mean – you're not referring to – *the* Jack Frost?' said Elsie. 'The one who's supposed to – what – bring the ice and snow?'

'That's him,' said Maureen. 'I was wondering why we haven't had a thaw. He must be somewhere in the forest. Probably hiding out in that ice box on skis he's so proud of. With that bad-tempered reindeer in tow.'

'Perfect place to lie low, the forest. Especially in the snow, in a white house,' said Shirley, adding, 'He's on the run because he's wanted for questioning. That's what I heard.'

'Too right' said Maureen. 'He's gone too far this time. Abusing his powers and mistreating people like that. Caused a permanent winter in a forest in another dimension that lasted for a whole year. The poor animals and people who lived there were either half-buried or near solidly frozen when they were dug out from all that snow.' Elsie and Joey listened to all of this with wide-eyed astonishment. 'People are furious,' added Maureen.

'So they should be,' said Wendy. 'He needs a spell behind bars, that one.'

'I didn't think Jack Frost was real,' said Joey. 'I thought he was made up, like the Tooth Fairy or the Sandman or . . . or Old Man River.'

'What makes you think they're made up?' said Shirley. 'I happen to know the Tooth Fairy, we're in the same book club. Natasha de Minty, lives in an ivory castle. People call her Gnasher. Not to her face, mind.'

All three witches tittered.

'The Sandman's really popular,' Maureen told them. 'Well, everyone likes a good night's sleep. And I saw Old Man River in the laundrette last week, watching his smalls go round.'

'They're real all right,' said Shirley. 'Just because you've got a magical power doesn't mean you don't need to do normal things like eat or wash.'

'The Sandman doesn't wash,' corrected Maureen. 'He rubs himself down.'

'How do you get a magical power?' asked Joey. 'Are they just . . . randomly given out?'

'Handed down through the family,' Maureen told him. 'So don't hold out hopes for yourself,' she added, not unkindly.

'They love to flaunt their power around, some of the big names,' said Shirley. 'None are as bad as Jack, though. Goes round doing exactly what he likes. Builds flashy palaces all over the place that he doesn't even live in. And that silly all-white outfit he swaggers around in. Those daft white boots. That hat.'

'Vain as they come,' agreed Wendy.

'Only eats frozen food,' said Shirley. 'Takes ice baths. Rides around in his own weather system. Right through the middle of someone's summer.'

'And him with twelve children,' tutted Wendy. 'Very bad influence on them, he is.'

'His wife's all right, though,' observed Shirley.

'What, Mrs Frost? Yes, very nice woman,' agreed Wendy. 'Sensible. Stays home with the kids and gets on with things while Jack rides around causing havoc and refusing to abide by the rules of the Magic Circle. They've given him enough warnings.'

'There's a Magic Circle? With rules?' asked Elsie. This was all new and rather interesting.

'Of course. Someone has to be in charge. Where magic's concerned, you've got to be sensible or there'd be chaos.'

'Who's in the Magic Circle?' Joey asked.

'No one knows.' Wendy lowered her voice. 'It's top secret. There are thirteen of them. A wizard, a gnome, a troll, you know, all the main magical factions are represented. I might be in it, as the witch representative, for example, but I couldn't say.'

'You're not, though,' said Shirley.

'I might be.'

'You're not, though.'

'Well, *whoever's* in it, it's time they did something about Jack,' said Maureen. 'They need to catch him and bring him in and bang him up until he promises to stop making endless winters and freezing everything and making poor little old ladies fall over.'

'You don't – you don't think he has anything

to do with Magenta disappearing, do you?' asked Elsie.

All three witches shook their heads.

'Jack Frost doesn't bother with us witches,' said Maureen. 'And us witches aren't especially bothered by him. But he's best avoided, especially as he's on the run. That makes him dangerous. Take our advice, Elsie. Stop worrying about Magenta. Witches can take care of themselves. When you get back to the tower, concentrate on keeping warm. Keep the fire banked up. Lock the doors and shutters. Keep the cold out.'

'That's right,' chorused Wendy and Shirley. 'Keep the cold out.'

'Once it's in, it's hard to make it leave,' added Shirley. 'So don't let it in.'

Chapter Eight
LOST

Sylphine wasn't much of a tracker. She liked skipping about at random in nature, not following a trail, where you have to concentrate. Mind you, her floaty scarves got tangled in bushes and her hair collected leaves and twigs whatever she did in the forest – track, dance, skip, walk, or simply stand still and breathe.

As well as losing her hat, it wasn't long before Sylphine lost two of the scarves and was . . . well, lost. Following footprints in the snow was easy enough when they clearly led in one direction, but when she reached the glade where everyone had stopped for a snowball fight, the place was one huge, confused, churned up mess. She tried following various sets of tracks leading away through the trees, but they either faded out or doubled back on themselves. It was all down to finding the right set – the ones that would lead her to the witch's cottage.

On her fourth return to the glade, Sylphine found a promising set of paw marks. She had a good feeling about them. She was *sure* they were the right ones. She was wrong, which leads us on to what happened next.

I must have been doing this for over an hour, thought Sylphine, *and finally I've found the right tracks that will clearly lead to – oh no. They're fading! I've gone and got it all wrong again . . . what is THAT?* She stopped short, with a gasp.

A short way ahead lay a clearing. Tall trees stood in a rough circle around a large, frozen lake. Parked next to the lake was . . . a sleigh with a house on!

Sylphine, like Nuisance before her, had never seen anything like the

vehicle in front of her. Her eyes widened as she took it in: the whiteness, the teeth-like icicles, the black windows, the way the runners reared up. The sleigh had an air of danger combined with a vast amount of showing off.

It suddenly seemed to be getting very cold. Sylphine shivered and rubbed her hands together. Her nose started to hurt, so she rubbed that too. Then a movement caught her eye . . .

A huge, dark, heavily-antlered head poked out of the trees, followed by an unpleasant, harsh jangling as the rest of the creature followed.

Sylphine's mouth dropped open. A reindeer!

Now, despite Sylphine's great love for them, animals didn't really take to Sylphine. She was just a bit . . . pushy and over keen. Treating them like pets when they were wild: giving them extra-rich food that upset their bellies, dragging them off on 'walkies', hugging them, expecting them to pose in the background and add extra loveliness while she did her moonlight dancing. The smaller ones – squirrels and mice and tiny tortoises and so on – she actually danced *with*. She had been known to dress up hedgehogs in bonnets and put ribbons on rabbits. Nobody likes being used as a prop.

Ohhhhh, thought Sylphine. *I love it!*

Well. Of course she did. Who doesn't love a reindeer, with its strength and speed and glamorous silhouette and amazing antlers? Everyone loves the amazing antlers, don't they? Sylphine took one look and melted.

I want you, she thought. *You can come home with me and live in my garden for ever.*

Well. Who wouldn't want a reindeer, with its strength and speed and—? Actually, most people, I should imagine. You might *love* a reindeer but you wouldn't really *want it*. Who would clear up after it? Or feed it when you were away on holiday? Wouldn't it take up too much space? Mightn't it skewer you on its amazing antlers? But Sylphine wasn't most people and didn't think like that.

She should have known better, of course. Not that long ago, there had been an incident with a unicorn in a magical emporium that hadn't gone well. Large, muscular animals with sharp pointy things growing out of their heads were probably best avoided by Sylphine. But when she fell for an animal, she fell hard.

Of course, the reindeer clearly wasn't wandering free. Sylphine could see that it was employed to pull the weird-looking house on runners.

I bet the cruel owners treat it mean, thought Sylphine. *Hanging those horrible bells around its neck for a start.*

The reindeer stood in the middle of the glade. The evil bells jangled tunelessly as it eyed Sylphine, chewing slowly on a mouth full of moss.

Sylphine approached at a half crouch, hand extended encouragingly.

'Hello, Mister Reindeer,' she said, using her special low, soothing, trust-me-I'm-a-friend-of-all-animals voice. 'I'm Sylphine and I'm a friend of all animals. Do you like oats? I've got oats in my garden. Have you got a name? Do you know anyone called Rudolph, or is that just a made-up story? Come on, Mister Reindeer, don't be shy—'

'Whachoo doin'?' said a voice from behind.

Sylphine gave a startled yelp and whirled around. Staring at her from under the low, snow-filled branches of a tree was a girl.

She was probably around the same age as Sylphine, but there the resemblance ended. This girl wasn't trying to look like a wood sprite. Definitely not floaty or dancy. Instead she was slouchy and slumpy. She had a long nose and a down-turned mouth. Her hair was mouse-brown and stuck out at weird angles. She wore a shapeless tunic and baggy trousers with sagging pockets. Her hands were stuffed into the pockets and her feet were rammed into down-at-heel shoes.

'I . . . I was just saying hello to this reindeer,' said Sylphine.

'Why?'

'Because . . . well, I love him.'

'He don't love *you*, though, do he?'

It was true. The reindeer was moving away, giving Sylphine dirty looks over its shoulder. At least the evil bells weren't so close, which was a relief.

'Is he yours?' asked Sylphine. 'Do you live in that weird house on skis?'

'None o' your business.'

'What do you call the reindeer?'

'Not tellin'.'

'Why not?' said Sylphine. 'I just want to make him like me. It's easier to be friendly when

you know someone's name. Mine's Sylphine Greenmantle. What's yours?'

'Oh,' said the girl. She sounded surprised. 'Um, I'm Tracy. He's called Spike. He don't like nobody, actually, except Ma. It's not just you.'

'If you took those bells off he'd be happier,' said Sylphine.

'How do you know?'

'Because I know all about animals. I have a way with them.' Sylphine peered around the silent clearing. The ice house's sinister black windows stared back, like eyes. 'Brrr. It's a bit spooky round here. You don't live in that nasty sleigh thing on your own, do you?'

'It's an ice house. Don't let Dad hear you callin' it names, he built it himself. He uses it for when he needs to get away.'

'What, for a holiday?'

'No. Get away. You know. Smartish.'

Tracy looked uncomfortable, so Sylphine changed the subject.

'Did you say you've got brothers? How many?'

As an only child, Sylphine liked the sound of brothers. She thought she'd like three, ideally. Three brothers. Free brothers. Three brothers who were free, like the wind. Brothers who would go dancing over hills, scattering petals romantically and probably singing.

'Two here. Trev and Terry. They're twins.' Tracy told her. 'But I got nine more back home.'

'*Nine?*'

'Yeah. They all gets on my nerves but not as much as Trev and Terry. I wish I'd stayed back in the palace with Ma. She said I wouldn't like it on the run and I don't. It's squashed an' everythin's made of ice and the shower's cold and Dad won't even allow a hot water bottle.' Tracy stuck out her lip and kicked at the snow. 'He is soooo annoying. Never lets me do nuffin'.'

'Did you say – back in the palace?' asked Sylphine.

'Yeah, we've got loads of *palaces* but we can't use 'em because there'll be people there waiting for Dad to show up and he don't want to talk to 'em. Me and the boys live in just the one. The comfy one Ma pays for.'

'Fancy having lots of palaces! Even if you only live in one,' said Sylphine. 'You're lucky. Wait . . . what did you mean by "on the run"?'

'Don't tell anyone, right? Fact is, Dad's in a bit of trouble. He's got his eye on some magical movin' tower that's supposed to be somewhere round here. We haven't found it yet. Well, Trev did, then he lost it again. When we do find it, we'll be moving in right away.'

Sylphine tried not to gasp, squeal or blink. She went red, took a deep breath and spoke carefully.

'I see. Does the owner know this?'

'Dad says she's not there.'

'Oh. Right. Um . . . why does your dad want a tower? In particular?'

'So 'e can take off to annuver dimension. Now fings are gettin' a bit, you know, hot.'

'Mm. And what will happen to the ice house when you've all gone to live in another dimension, in this, er, tower?'

'Spike'll take it home to Ma's and she'll stick it back in the garage for when Dad needs it again. Which he won't if the tower works out.'

'I see. You don't suppose Spike would like to come and live with me?'

'Nah. He likes it back at Ma's, she throws his bells in the bin and gives him chocolate biscuits.'

'Fair enough,' said Sylphine, with a regretful little sigh.

'Do you like blue?' asked Tracy suddenly.

'I do. But my best is green,' said Sylphine. She loved talking about favourite colours. 'Wood sprites wear green. Blue would suit *you*, though.'

'I fink green's nice too,' said Tracy. 'Almost as good as blue. Dad's always wantin' me to wear white, cos we're the Frosts. I won't, though. He always wears white in public. Likes to make a splash.'

'Oh, you don't want to splash white,' said Sylphine. 'One spill's all it takes.'

'I know,' said Tracy. 'I told him that.'

The two of them stood and stared at each other.

'You got lots o' nice curly hair,' Tracy said.

'Have I?' said Sylphine, delighted. She reached up and patted her unwashed locks. 'It's not at its best right now. I've run out of shampoo.'

'I use Spike's saddle soap,' the girl informed her. 'When I can be bovvered.'

'Oh, but you mustn't!' cried Sylphine. 'You'll strip away all the natural oils. Saddle soap is too harsh for hair. I use a special shampoo that—'

'What did you say your name was?'

'Sylphine Greenmantle.'

'Did you make that up?'

Sylphine considered. Should she admit to really being Aggie Wiggins? Or should she lie? She would lie.

'No. Of course not.'

'You did, though, dincha?' said Tracy. For the first time, she smiled. Her blue eyes crinkled up.

She looked much friendlier. 'That's all right, it's nice. If I made up *my* own name it'd be Crystal-Louise. Crystal-Louise Frost.'

'That's lovely,' said Sylphine, meaning it. She imagined being friends with Tracy, sitting down together doing each other's hair and making lists of lovely girls' names.

'Or Snowdrop Isobelle Marina,' said Tracy. 'Or Cindy Sparkle. Or Tiara Porchetta-Diamonti.'

She's given it a lot of thought, Sylphine noted to herself. *Like I did*. 'I like Crystal-Louise best,' she told Tracy. 'You could dye your hair blue, to go with your eyes.'

'You fink?'

Just then, there came a sharp shout.

'Oi! Trace! Dad says, who're you talkin' to?'

Two identical figures came striding

purposefully across the snow. Both of them wore long, flapping white coats, flat white caps and, of all things, white shoes with pointy toes. Beneath the coats were rather grubby-looking white waistcoats. Both had pale, pinched faces and big ears.

'Here they come,' said Tracy, with a sniff. 'The twins. Always spoilin' everyfing. D'you really mean it, about my hair?'

But she was talking to thin air.

★ ★ ★ ★

'I'm starving,' said Joey, as they made their way back through the forest. Nuisance and Bill were keeping close, clearly happy to be going back to the tower.

'I'd magic you a chocolate egg if my fingers

weren't so cold,' said Elsie. 'We'll get things from the larder when we get back. And decide what to do nex—'

'Elsieeee! Joeeeeee!' broke in a voice. 'It's meeeeee!'

Nuisance gave a little bark of recognition as a dishevelled figure came stumbling through the trees.

'Aggie!' cried Joey. 'What are you doing here?'

Sylphine came puffing up, trailing her torn blanket through the snow.

'*There* you are! I came looking for you but I got lost and there was a reindeer called Spike and this weird ice house and I met someone called Tracy but then her brothers shouted and I ran! I think they're planning to steal the tower! And it's *Sylphine*, Joey, as you well know!' Sylphine threw herself into Elsie's arms, nearly knocking her off balance. 'Oh, Elsie! I'm so glad to see you! Will you make me some shampoo? And oh, I'm *hungry*!'

'There, there,' said Elsie, patting her friend on the back. Customer Service Rule Five was really coming in handy lately. 'Calm down. Who's Tracy?'

'Tracy Frost. She washes her hair in saddle soap.'

Elsie and Joey exchanged a look.

'Let's all walk back to the tower for lunch and you can tell us all about it on the way,' said Elsie.

Chapter Nine
THE FROSTS

Meanwhile, two lanky figures stood in the snowy clearing, staring up at the tower. Terry and Trevor Frost had come to snoop around on the orders of their dad.

The tower had taken them a while to find, even with the advantage of daylight, but finally the twins had come across the trail of footprints left by Trevor the night before and back-tracked to the glade. They were now in the middle of a shouted conversation with an unfriendly black bird glaring down at them from the roof.

'Where's the witch, blackbird?' shouted Trevor.

'None of your business, sonny,' squawked Corbett. 'And for your information, I am the resident *raven*. R.A.V.E.N. *Not* a blackbird. We're different.'

'We finks she's gone,' said Terry. 'It's just you in there, livin' a sad little birdy life on yer own.'

'Wrong,' said Corbett. 'I'm expecting her back any d— moment. In fact . . . Yes, I think I can hear her downstairs now.'

'Oh yeah? Let's see her, then. Oi! Witch! Come out!'

They waited. Nothing happened.

'Tell the truth, birdy' shouted Terry. 'It's obvious you're lying through yer beak. This tower's empty!'

'If you really must know, Witch Sharp has been delayed and Witch Pickles is temporarily taking over!' snapped Corbett. 'Not that I need to explain things to the likes of you. What are you up to anyway? Snooping around here with your nosy questions?'

'Tell the birdy what we're up to, Trev,' said Terry.

'We're gonna take this tower over,' said Trevor. 'We're movin' in. And we can, because our dad said.'

'Your dad being?' asked Corbett.

'Jack Frost. *The* Jack Frost.'

'He's a legend,' added Terry.

'Not a good one, though,' said Corbett. 'Most people think he's a thieving bully who doesn't deserve a magical power. But why am I wasting my time talking to you? Go away and don't come back. You don't want to be here when Witch Pickles arrives.'

With that he vanished below the parapet.

Terry and Trevor looked at each other.

'Dad said it was empty,' said Terry. 'Ripe for the taking.'

'He's not gonna be happy,' said Trevor. 'It sounds like there's a back-up witch. As well as that gobby bird.'

'The bird don't count, though. It's the witch that counts, innit?'

'Yeah, well, whatever. It'll put him in a right mood.' Trev sighed heavily.

'I didn't like that tower much,' said Terry as they turned and trudged away. He glanced uneasily over his shoulder. 'Giving off unfriendly vibes, it was. I don't think it wants us to move in.'

'The ivy's nice,' said Trevor.

'Yeah, it's *pretty* enough,' conceded Terry, 'but there can't be much space in there. Dad'll take the biggest room and give the next best to Tracy and we'll get to share a cupboard. And there'll be loads of stairs. It's a tower, innit? Tall and thin.'

'Maybe it's magically bigger on the inside than the outside,' suggested Trev. 'Some places are. But it's not the looks what count, is it? It's the movin' bit that counts. First sign o' danger, shove off to a different dimension, problem sorted. I heard these towers have got other special features as well. Some of 'em have a magic larder wiv all yer favourite food.'

'That'd be good,' said Trevor. 'Better than what Dad cooks.'

'He don't cook it, though,' said his twin. 'It's

all frozen. I could do wiv a decent hot meal, like Ma makes.'

'Don't say that in front of 'im,' said Trevor. 'We'll get anuvver lecture about how we're the Frosts and we Don't Do Hot.' He stopped and looked around. 'Are we goin' the right way?'

'I fink so. I recognizes that tree.'

Uncertainly, they moved on.

'I'll tell you somefing, Trev,' said Terry. 'I wish I hadn't come. Dad reckons he's doing us a favour, showin' us 'is lifestyle, 'ow he does what he wants an' takes what he wants an' lives by 'is own set o' rules. But I'm not that interested in 'avin' a magical power. I don't want to bring winter. I'd sooner learn a trade.'

'Me too,' said Trevor. 'I've certainly 'ad enough of that ice house.'

'I've 'ad enough of Dad,' said Terry. 'Shoutin'

an' bossin' us about. An' makin' us wear these daft white coats and caps and white shoes. Whoever wears white shoes in winter?'

'Too right,' said Trevor mournfully, as they trudged along through the snow.

Some distance away, inside the ice house, another conversation was taking place through a closed bathroom door made of ice. Jack Frost was talking to his daughter.

'Tracy,' said Jack. 'Stop sulkin'.'

'You never let me do nuffin',' came the sullen mumble from behind the door.

'I do, darlin', I do. I spoils you rotten. Remember that little penguin I gotcha?'

'You mean the one you took away because it did a whoopsy in your stupid boot?'

'They're Daddy's special boots, though, ain't they? That's why Daddy was a bit cross. What about the nice frock I got you for yer birthday?'

'It was white! I hate white! I like green and I quite like pink but I like blue best and you don't even *know*. You're mean. Why can't I have a friend?'

'What d'you need a friend for when you got family? You're a Frost!'

'So what? If I can't see Sylphine then we might as well go back to Ma's!'

'We can't go back to Ma's because I'm havin' a little bit o' bovver wiv the authorities. You knew that when you came wiv me. You begged me to let you come.'

'I thought it'd be fun, but it's not. I'm cold and bored and the food's horrible.'

'Well, we're gonna live in a magic movin' tower soon. Once yer dozy brothers find it again, we'll be moving in. You'll love it. We'll whizz about all over the place! We'll set off a few avalanches! Build more ice palaces! Or just go somewhere chilly and watch old people fall over. Your choice.'

'I don't want to go all over the place, I just want to go to Sylphine Greenmantle's and dye my hair blue. You never let me do nuffin'.'

Jack spun round in his chair, pointed a finger at the wall and let off a single exasperated blast of ice. It drilled through the wall in a shower of white and blue sparks, making quite a decent-sized hole. Through it, he caught a glimpse of Spike in the distance, looking angry.

'I heard that,' came the voice behind the bathroom ice door. 'Ma says you shouldn't use your frosting finger indoors. When I get home, I'm telling.'

Chapter Ten
NOW WHAT?

Back at the tower, everyone sat in the kitchen with their toes thawing, tucking into a late lunch, courtesy of the magic larder. Sylphine had jelly and cake; Joey was halfway through a bowl of jammy rice pudding. Elsie had gone for a cheese sandwich and Corbett was picking at a plate full of nuts and raisins, with a side order of spiders sprinkled with icing sugar. Outside, on the doorstep, Nuisance was eating a sausage, watched with vague horror by Bill.

(Wire baskets don't eat.)

Nobody talked much until the food was gone. All that walking through the snowy forest had been tiring – and though no one wanted to admit it out loud, they hadn't really achieved much.

Corbett was bursting to tell everyone about the Frost boys' visit, but had so far refrained, although it was making his beak ache. Nobody had asked him how his day had gone, he noticed. He would spring it on them. A big reveal, when they were really paying attention.

'So, the witches didn't help at all?' he said.

'No,' said Joey. 'They didn't seem a bit bothered about Her Witchiness going missing. More keen to talk about Jack Frost.'

'Oh yes?' Corbett looked casual. 'Jack Frost, eh? What about him?'

'It seems he's in the forest,' said Elsie. 'He's got three of his children with him. Sylphine saw them, didn't you, Sylphine?'

Sylphine scraped up the last of her jelly. 'I did. There's a reindeer called Spike and they live in a scary ice house on runners. And I talked to Tracy, she's his daughter, then her brothers came out and I ran away. Tracy said they want to move into the tower, but they can't, can they? Tracy was nice, though.'

'What did she say exactly about her dad being in trouble?' asked Elsie.

'Nothing much. Just that he's on the run and they can't go home. You'll never guess where home is.'

This was Corbett's moment. He had remained silent for long enough.

'Could be any of many flashy ice palaces

dotted around in various cold dimensions,' he said. 'All space and echoes, no soft furnishings. Ice statues and carvings everywhere. Massive grounds with frozen lakes. All for show, of course. Nobody lives in any of them except a yeti called Ian. He's the caretaker.'

'Corbett!' cried Elsie. 'How do you know so much about Jack Frost's living arrangements?'

'Well, nobody bothered to ask about *my* day,' said Corbett, 'but it so happens I had quite an interesting morning. After the Frost boys had come and gone, I went up to Magenta's office—'

'Whoah!' shouted Elsie and Joey, in chorus.

Corbett ignored them and continued, '– and I looked up Jack Frost in *Who's What*? It gives little potted histories about all the big names. Also –' he paused, and gave a proud little smirk, enjoying his moment – 'I happen to know an eagle called Neville who is mates with Ian. They play darts together. After looking up Jack, I flew off and had a word with Nev.'

'Go back to the start,' said Joey. 'What was that about the Frost boys being here?'

'Oh, didn't I say? They called round earlier. Snooping around, demanding to see the witch, who *wasn't here.*' He stared pointedly at Elsie.

'We tried to be quick,' said Elsie.

'Well, anyway, Sylphine's right, Jack is planning to seize the tower. Somehow, he's found out that the tower is without a witch.'

'Did you tell them Elsie's here, covering for Magenta?' said Sylphine.

'I did,' said Corbett. 'But I suspect Jack will think—' He caught Joey's eye and closed his beak.

'What?' said Elsie.

'Nothing.'

'You think he'll assume I won't be able to stop him?' said Elsie. 'That I'll be a walkover for someone like him?'

'Well, he knows a few tricks, Elsie. He's been around for a while.'

'And I'm still in training.'

'You're getting good, though,' said Sylphine loyally. 'We all have faith in you, don't we, Joey?'

''Course we do,' said Joey, who had been saying little because he was busy eating. 'Out of interest, Corbs, in all those palaces, is everything made of frost and ice? Even the toilets?'

'There aren't any toilets. Everything's just for show,' said Corbett. 'Nowhere to boil a kettle, even.'

'How does Ian manage, then?' asked Joey. 'With no kettle or toilet?'

'Neville didn't say. But he did say that Jack's wife hates all of Jack's palaces. That's why she has her own and decorated it herself. Heavy velvet curtains and roaring fires and draft excluders. Lots of cushions. That sort of thing. In fact, she's not happy with Jack full-stop. Thinks he's a bad influence on the kids.'

'Wow, Corbett,' said Joey. 'I didn't know birds gossiped.'

'*I* don't. Nev does. I just listen and learn.' Corbett swallowed the last iced spider. 'Anyway Jack'll get what he deserves when the Magic Circle finally catches up with him. Let's not worry about him for now. We need to find Magenta. That's what's important.'

Elsie sighed. 'I just don't know what to do next. Thanks for your help, Joey and Sylphine, but you should probably both think about going home soon. It gets dark early with this snow.'

'I'm not going anywhere,' said Joey. 'Not with the Frosts lurking about making threats. Me and Bill are staying right here with you.'

'I'm staying, too,' said Sylphine. 'I don't want to go out in the cold again. I lost all my scarves. And sleepovers are fun!'

'Thanks,' said Elsie, pleased that she would have company.

'So, what shall we do next?' asked Joey.

But no one knew the answer to that.

Chapter Eleven
NOISES IN THE NIGHT

Later that evening, and after lots of discussion, they were still no further with a plan to track down Magenta.

Everyone was sitting together in the kitchen. Joey and Bill were tending to the fire, making sure the room stayed warm and cosy. Sylphine had found paper and crayons and was at the table drawing Spike from memory, surrounded by red hearts. Meanwhile, Elsie was looking through Magenta's spell books. Wendy, Shirley and Maureen might think that there was no point using magic to track down Magenta, but there was no harm in looking. But in the end, she gave up. None of the spells were right. They were all about finding where you'd left your glasses, your umbrella, your false teeth, things like that. Nothing at all about how to find a missing witch.

Corbett just couldn't settle. He didn't want to talk. He kept shuffling up and down his perch, shaking his head and giving huge sighs. The longer Magenta was missing, the more convinced he was that she had left because of him.

When the light began to fade, Elsie went out to feed Nuisance his supper sausage.

'Are you sure you'll be all right out here?' she whispered in his ear.

Nuisance gave her ear a lick. Yep. He would.

Elsie gave him a goodnight hug, spread out his bedding on the doorstep and took a look around the cold, silent glade. The moon was up, causing long blue shadows to creep across the snow. She went back in and locked and bolted the door.

In the kitchen, Corbett was on the far side of his perch,

head beneath his wing. Joey was snoozing in the rocking chair with Bill purring gently on his lap. Sylphine was asleep at the table, her head on her drawing.

Everything felt like it was in the right place. Except for the rightful witch.

I wish she'd come back, thought Elsie.

She collected blankets from the linen chest, and put them over her sleeping friends. She turned off the lamp and blew out the candles. Then she sat in the one remaining chair and pulled a blanket over herself. The bed upstairs in her own blue room was wonderful. But tonight, they needed to stay together.

There's no way I can sleep, she thought, *staring into the glowing fire. Not with everything that's going on. No way . . .*

Elsie awoke with a snap in the dark, the sound of jangling bells ringing in her ear.

For a moment, she thought she was back home in the flat, then she remembered where she was. She was in a chair in the tower kitchen and outside, Nuisance was barking.

He never barked at night. Something – or somebody – was out there.

Despite being banked high, the fire was almost out. Only a few embers still glowed orange. The kitchen felt cold.

'Do you hear that?' hissed Corbett, from out of the dark. 'Someone's out there. The tower knows it too. It's on alert. Feel it?'

Yes. Elsie *could* feel it. There was a definite feeling of tension in the air. The tower was clearly on edge.

'What's up?' came Joey's voice from

the armchair.

'There's someone outside,' said Elsie. 'I'm going to find out who.'

'I'm not sure that's a good idea,' said Corbett.

'Maybe not, but we can't leave Nuisance out there going mad all night.' The blanket slithered down as she stood up and groped for the matches.

'What's happening?' came Sylphine's bleary voice.

'I'm just taking a look outside,' said Elsie. A match flared and the wick of the big kitchen lamp caught the flame.

'I'm coming with you,' said Joey. 'Mind out, Bill, I'm standing up.'

'Me too,' said Sylphine.

Corbett flew onto her shoulder. 'We're all with you,' he said.

Followed
closely by
the others,
Elsie took
the lamp,
stepped
into the
tiny hall,
unlocked
the door
and
pulled
back the
bolts.

'Slowly,' advised Corbett. 'Just a crack.'

'No,' said Elsie. 'I want to see what we're dealing with.'

And she pulled the door wide open.

'Mumbling magpies!' squawked Corbett as the freezing air rushed in, blowing the lamp out. 'Steady on, it's blowing off my tail feathers!'

Outside, Nuisance was stiff-legged and bristling with fury. He looked at Elsie with frantic eyes and delivered his loudest bark yet.

'Thanks, Nuisance,' said Elsie. 'Good boy for sounding the alarm. We're here now.'

The forest glade was empty and bathed in starlight. So many stars, cold and distant, splashed across the night sky. Everything was black and white – shadows and snow.

'Who's there?' shouted Elsie. She put the lamp down on the doorstep. 'Show yourself, please.'

She used her Shopkeeper Voice, the one her dad used when he'd had a bad day in the Emporium and his back hurt and a customer was taking half an hour choosing a pencil. It was clear, polite, firm. You wouldn't want to argue with it.

There was a long pause, filled with nothing but silence. A cold wind sighed in the treetops and then . . . once again . . . there came the sound of cracked, jangling bells mixed in with a slithering noise and the cracking of snapping branches. From the cover of the trees came Spike the reindeer, pulling the ice house.

He stopped in the middle of the glade, shook his antlered head and bared his yellow teeth. The bells went silent. Behind him, the ice house glittered in starlight.

'Wow!' breathed Joey. '*Somebody's* out to make an impression. Just look at the size of that reindeer.'

'That's Spike,' Sylphine told him. 'I love him.'

Everyone waited for the next bit.

The door swung open. And Jack Frost stepped down into the snow.

Chapter Twelve
JACK

Elsie had imagined Jack Frost as tall and thin, with sticking-up hair and clothes cut in zigzags.

Joey had imagined someone tall and broad-shouldered, with a long cloak and flowing silver hair. A bit like Old Father Time, but younger.

Sylphine had rather hoped he would be glittery and elf-like, with pointy toes and a crystal crown.

So Jack Frost in the flesh was a bit of a disappointment for all of them.

He wasn't tall, for a start. In fact, he would

have been shorter than average if it wasn't for his white, pointy-toed, high-heeled knee boots. He wore a long white coat with a big fur collar. Rings glittered on every finger, and every finger ended in a long, sharp, silver nail. He had a small, pointy-ended moustache and long, greased-back white hair that he wore in a ponytail. On top of his head was a tall top hat, also white.

Nothing really went together. All you could say of it was that it was colour co-ordinated.

He stared at the little group crowded in the tower doorway.

'Hah! Just a bunch o' silly kids. And there was I, expecting a witch,' he said.

'Tell him,' Corbett said to Elsie.

'The witch is right here,' said Elsie. She spoke with no hesitation. She was the witch. 'Hello,

Mr Frost. I heard you were in the forest.'

I've come across your sort before, she thought. *You're the customer who strides past the queue and demands to be served first.*

'Is that right?' Jack raised an eyebrow. 'And there was me tryin' to be inconspicuous. That's what 'appens when you're a big name. People notice.'

'Show off,' hissed Sylphine into Joey's ear.

'I'm Elsie Pickles, Witch Sharp's stand-in,' Elsie told him. 'She's not available right now.'

'A bit of a titch for a witch, aincha?' Jack Frost stared insultingly. 'Where's yer pointy hat?'

'Witchcraft's not about size or hats,' said Elsie firmly. 'It's about reading the instructions, following the recipe and making it work.'

'That's right, you tell him,' encouraged Corbett.

'Don't let him bully you,' agreed Joey.

'I thought he'd be sparklier,' whispered Sylphine. 'And taller.'

'Look, please hurry up and say what you want

or we're going in,' said Elsie. 'It's the middle of the night and it's freezing.'

'All right,' said Jack, 'Let's talk business. I'm 'ere because I 'appen to be in need of specialist housin' requirements, in particular the ability to move off sharpish. Magenta Sharp's famous moving tower'll do me nicely. A little bird told me she's disappeared and it's up for grabs.'

'That'll be Nev,' said Corbett. 'Spread it around the bird population. Just can't keep his beak shut. I told him to keep it under his wing.'

'So I'm here for a viewing,' went on Jack. 'See how it works. If I like it, I'll be movin' in.'

'The tower's not up for grabs,' said Elsie, 'You can't take it over because there's a witch in it.'

'*You?*' sneered Jack. 'Hah! Move out the way, girl, I'm comin' in.' He took a step forward.

'Stay where you are,' said Elsie. 'We don't

want things to get unpleasant.'

'You're *threatenin'* me?' scoffed Jack. 'You want to test my magical power against a handful of puny kiddy spells?'

'Elsie's spells aren't puny!' shouted Joey. 'They're good!'

'She can do chocolate eggs!' piped up Sylphine, not that helpfully.

'Oh, oh, I'm so *scared*.' Jack clutched his head and staggered. 'Save me from the *chocolate eggs*!'

'You won't like the frog rain!' said Joey. 'Nobody does.'

'And she can freeze people!' added Sylphine, unwisely. 'I've seen her do it!'

'She can *freeze people*?' Jack Frost's eyebrows shot up. 'Do you know who you're talkin' to? I'm Jack Frost! *The* Jack Frost! I'll show you freezin'! I can make your little pink noses turn blue and drop off! Make the ice crack when you go skating! Bury you in an avalanche! *I bring winter!*'

'We've noticed,' said Elsie, 'but it's gone on too long.'

'Girly,' said Jack Frost. 'I am through with messin' about!'

He took another step closer.

This was too much for Nuisance. All this time he had kept the barks back and swallowed the growls and put a lid on the frenzied jumping. But this was too hard to take. This nasty man was threatening Elsie and he wasn't having it.

He flew forward, barking and snarling and growling and really giving it everything he had.

'Nuisance!' shouted Elsie, worried how Jack would react. 'No! Don't!'

Jack Frost pointed a long, sharp index finger.

From the tip spurted a
white, dazzling stream
of frost! It hit Nuisance
squarely in the chest as
he jumped. There
was a crackling
sound, and he
froze in mid-
air. Stiffened,
whitened,
hardened – and
fell heavily into
the snow with a crunch.

Bill left his place at
Joey's ankles and launched
himself into the air, making a
beeline for his doggy friend. Basket
to the rescue!

'Bill!' yelled Joey, jumping from the doorway. 'Don't do it!'

Too late. Two more streams of frost shot from two extended fingers. One struck Bill dead centre. Frost snaked along the wires, turning them silvery white. Bill drifted down to the snow like a broken butterfly. The second stream struck Joey in the shoulder. Crackling white tendrils of frost snapped across his face and around his body. He stiffened, then crashed face-first into the snow.

'You beast!' squealed Sylphine. 'If you've hurt them, you mean, nasty m—'

To Elsie and Corbett's horror, a fourth stream of silver frost zapped Sylphine. She froze on the spot then slowly keeled over sidewise. Only the door frame kept her from falling.

'Now, *that*, small witch,' said Jack, 'is freezin'.'

'That was really mean,' said Elsie in her steeliest voice. The cold, angry one she used with shoplifters. 'Why on earth did you have to do that? I'm not surprised that the Magic Circle are after you.'

'So?' said Jack. 'They ain't caught me yet. They'll 'ave no chance at all when I'm in control of the tower. I'll be able to move off to another dimension where they can't get me. A nice cold, icy place . . . lovely! Now why don't you be a good little witch and show me round?'

'Don't!' hissed Corbett. 'Don't let him in!'

'Defrost my friends,' Elsie said. A plan was starting to form in her mind. 'Then maybe I'll let you inside and show you what the tower can do.'

'Terry?' shouted Jack. 'Trev? Job for yah! Some rubbish needs clearin' up. Stack 'em up and keep an eye on 'em. I'll defrost 'em later.'

'No,' said Elsie. 'Thaw them now, or no deal.'

'Terry? Defrost 'em, but don't let 'em scarper. Tie 'em up if you like.'

'No tying up,' said Elsie.

'Trev? No tyin' up.'

'Thank you,' said Elsie. 'Come in, Mr Frost.'

'*What?*' hissed Corbett from her shoulder.

'Sssh,' Elsie whispered to him. 'Trust me, okay?' She raised her voice. 'Wipe your boots, please, Mr Frost.'

And with that she picked up the lamp, turned and went in. Jack strode behind her, rudely elbowing Sylphine out of his way. Her frozen body fell sideways like a plank.

Chapter Thirteen
THE PERFECT DESTINATION

The kitchen was bitterly cold. The fire had gone out, of course, which didn't help, but Jack Frost brought his own, personal cold with him, too. He stood staring around, shaking snow off his white boots.

Elsie took some matches, lit the lamp again and placed it next to the sink. 'There, that's better. Now we can see,' she said.

Jack moved away from the flame. Even the small flicker of heat it gave out obviously made him uncomfortable.

Good, thought Elsie. *Just as I hoped.*

'So,' she said, turning to Jack. 'This is the kitchen. Small but with some useful inbuilt magical features. Keeps itself tidy. Washes up if you're really tired. Lays the table. Then there's the magic larder that will provide anything you want to eat.'

'Will it do mango an' cherry ice cream?'

'No,' said Corbett coldly. 'Not for you, it won't. May sparrows spit on your stupid hat.'

'Tell that bird to shut its beak. 'Ow many bedrooms?'

'Two. Do you want to see them?'

''Ow many steps?'

'Lots,' said Corbett. 'Too steep to climb in daft boots.'

'You're askin' for a frostin',' said Jack. 'I'm

warnin' you, bird.'

'You could use Witch Sharp's office if you need an extra bedroom,' went on Elsie. 'I don't know what you'll do with all her stuff. I suppose you could store it in the cellar.'

Corbett opened his beak to speak, then closed it again. He couldn't understand what was happening. Not only had Elsie let Jack Frost in, she was being extra helpful. He knew she liked her customer service rules, but Jack Frost wasn't a *customer*. He was a thief. Why help a thief?

'Get to the important bit. 'Ow do I make it move?'

'Well, you don't *make* it do anything,' said Elsie. 'It's more of a polite request kind of thing. Treat the tower with respect and it's happy to help. Always ask nicely and remember to say thank you.'

'That's it?' asked Jack. 'I just stand 'ere and tell it where I want to go?'

'Well, there's a bit more to it than that. There's a little ritual you need to go through. I'll show you, shall I?'

'*Elsie*!' croaked Corbett in her ear. 'What are you *playing* at?'

'Shush. Mr Frost wants to see the tower move and we're giving him a demonstration.' She raised her voice. 'Tower! Access to the Star Room, please!'

There was a pause. Then the walls vibrated. The kitchen rug rolled itself back to expose a large flagstone that detached itself from the surrounding stones and rose up and up and up to the ceiling, where it bobbed gently against a rafter.

'Uh-huh,' said Jack Frost. 'A secret slab what floats. Not bad. Now what?'

'Don't show him,' advised Corbett in her ear.

'Down to the Star Room in the basement,' said Elsie, ignoring the raven. 'Follow me.'

Elsie led the way down the steps, with Corbett on her shoulder, still grumbling urgently into her ear. Jack Frost came clumping down behind, complaining that there wasn't a handrail. His white high-heeled boots were clearly not made for stairs. Cobwebs brushed against his white coat.

At the bottom, a low passageway led away into the shadows.

'Lights, please, Tower!' said Elsie.

Instantly, tiny little dots of twinkling lights lined the passage walls.

'Right,' said Elsie. 'Keep your head down, the ceiling's low. Maybe start thinking about where you want to go? It's your first trip, so make it something to remember. Why don't you choose your ideal holiday destination? Where would that be, do you think?'

'Somewhere freezing, of course,' said Corbett with a sneer. 'Just for a change.'

'You're right, bird,' said Jack. 'That's what I like. A five-star ice hotel with big screens in all the rooms, showin' people fallin' over, en-suite frozen lake, fir trees, snow-capped mountains, big private Keep Out notices.'

'Perfect,' said Elsie. 'Keep that in mind. This is the best bit. The big reveal . . .'

They had reached the end of the passageway and all of a sudden the room before them was lit by thousands upon thousands of stars. Whirling and swirling above and around, shining silver against dark, dark blue. The floor beneath their feet changed into something white and wispy and cool, like the inside of a cloud, or a sandy beach in moonlight. And right in the middle of that starry sky was the large, silver, eight-spoked wheel, like that of a ship, spinning slowly in mid-air, giving off blue twinkles and sparkles.

'Oh, right,' said Jack. 'A magic wheel. I'm supposed to turn it, am I?'

'Yes,' said Elsie. 'Give it one full revolution, while stating slowly and clearly where you want to go. Don't jerk your hand away when the spokes heat up. Go on.'

'What d'you mean, spokes 'eat up?' Jack looked alarmed.

'The spokes get a bit hot. That's all.'

''Ow come?'

'I don't know. All part of the magic, I suppose.'

'You do it,' Jack told her.

'What? Why?'

'I'm not touchin' 'ot spokes. You do it.'

'All right, if you insist.'

With Corbett on her shoulder, Elsie stepped up to the wheel, which slowed to a standstill. She reached out and took hold of the two topmost spokes. She felt the usual pleasantly ticklish buzzing sensation in her hands.

'Tower,' said Elsie, 'this is Elsie. Please take me to the perfect holiday destination.'

Slowly, the wheel began to turn. The stars froze in their tracks. There came the sound of faraway tinkling bells and the distinct smell of roses. The wheel completed one full rotation and Elsie stepped back and waited for the last of the special effects, which came right on cue.

There was a sudden, dazzling explosion of white light, causing everyone to clap their hands over their eyes.

'What's 'appenin'?' shouted Jack.

'Calm down, Mr Frost,' said Elsie. 'You can open your eyes now. We've arrived.'

Jack opened his eyes. The three of them were standing at the foot of the stairs leading up to the kitchen. There were no stars, no lights, nothing. Just the normal stuff you would find in

a basement – broken furniture, old gardening
tools, cobwebs. In her hands, Elsie held an old
cartwheel.

'And that's the show the tower likes to put on when it moves,' she said, putting down the wheel. 'It's not exactly instant transportation, but very reliable. Let's go up and see where it's taken us.'

'I don't like all these stairs,' complained Jack, panting a bit as they climbed back up to the kitchen, where the flagstone still wobbled quietly up in the rafters.

'Probably best not to move into a tower with its controls in the basement, then,' Corbett snapped.

'Belt up, bird!' Jack drew a large white handkerchief from his coat pocket and dabbed at his brow. 'Phew! It was stuffy down there. I'm too warm.'

'Do you want a glass of water?' Elsie walked to the sink.

'Is it properly cold?' asked Jack.

'As cold as you'll get.'

'Yes, then.'

Elsie picked up a clean glass and turned on the tap. Behind the sink, on the kitchen windowsill, the solitary lamp still burned.

Now's my chance, thought Elsie. *How did that rhyme go again? Something like . . . hot and cold, cold and hot, come together, hit the spot.*

'What are you doing over there?' asked Jack, fanning himself with his top hat.

'Making sure it's cold enough. Here.'

Jack Frost took the glass from Elsie's hand. That was his first big mistake.

He took a huge swig. That was his second.

His eyes went huge. His face went red. Sweat began to stream down his face. His mouth opened wide and he sucked in air whilst pointing pitifully down his throat.

'Fresh air!' cried Elsie. 'Quick, the door!'

She ran into the hall and threw the door wide open. Jack staggered towards it.

That was his last big mistake.

Chapter Fourteen
EVERYTHING EXPLAINED

'That's when she pushed him!' crowed Corbett. 'It was brilliant! His face was like a tomato and he was lurching about, gasping and sweating and pointing down his throat and then Elsie opened the door and outside, instead of it being all wintry, it was blazing sunshine! All hot and nice with blue sea and white sand and coconut trees! The perfect tropical island!'

'*I get it*! It was *Elsie's* dream holiday destination, not Jack's!' said Sylphine. 'Because she was the one at the wheel. Yes?'

'You should have seen his face when he realized!' crowed Corbett. 'Jack Frost with his mouth on fire, stranded on a tropical island! My beak nearly fell off!'

'Well done, Elsie,' said Joey. 'Er – how did you make the water so hot?'

'Just the heat from the lamp.' Elsie explained. 'I've been practising a bit at home. ' She grinned. 'I guess I wanted to get into hot water.' They all burst out laughing.

It was early the following morning and Elsie, Joey, Sylphine and Corbett were sitting in the kitchen, eating pancakes and talking about the events of the night.

Outside, there were big changes. The sky was pale blue, the sun shone and the snow and frost were finally thawing. Water dripped from the trees and the white patches on the forest floor were growing smaller by the minute. There was no sign of the ice house, or the Frost children.

Nuisance and Bill sat quietly on the doorstep, both enjoying the warmth of the first ray of sunshine.

'At least there are lots of nice cool pools to drink from there,' said Elsie. 'I know, because it's my perfect holiday spot.'

'He won't be there long anyway,' said Corbett. 'He's a wanted man trapped on an island.'

'Well, he brought it all on himself by being so nasty,' said Sylphine. 'It's all gone wrong for him in the end, hasn't it?'

'That's what's supposed to happen when you're a baddy,' said Joey.

'It was so funny!' Corbett gave a smirk. 'I really enjoyed the tearing off of the clothes and running into the sea!'

'I did, too,' admitted Elsie, smiling. 'And I

quite liked it when he ducked under the palm tree for shade and the monkeys pelted him with coconuts!'

'I wish I'd seen that,' said Joey.

'We watched through the letterbox after we closed the door on him,' said Corbett. 'It was hilarious.'

'He deserves to get laughed at,' said Joey. 'Him and his silly boots. When the Magic Circle knows where he is, they'll arrest him and bring him in for questioning and he'll do some answering and unless he shows loads of humility and agrees to go to therapy, they'll confiscate his power. Right, Corbs?'

'Right,' agreed Corbett. 'Just think. The great Jack Frost, brought down by our Elsie.'

'Oh!' Sylphine gave little gasp. 'You don't think he'll be able to just summon up winter and escape that way, do you? On the back of the north wind or something?'

'Not a chance. He has to abide by the tower's rules,' explained Corbett: *'No magic power can interfere. The tower's power shall persevere.* Jack can't meddle with Elsie's dream holiday destination. He's stuck there 'til he's picked up.'

'So everything's getting sorted,' said Elsie happily. 'Jack's out of action, the snow's thawing and Spring's coming. And, best of all, Magenta's home!'

Oooh!

Well, now. You weren't expecting that, were you? Yes, Magenta is back! Shall we find out how *that* happened and fill in a few other details, while we're about it?

First, let's go back to the moment when the tower disappeared. Coincidentally, at the same *exact* moment, Magenta Sharp materialized in the glade. The air shivered, and there she was, her red hair, cloak, boots and gloves creating a bright splash against the white, moonlit snow. She took one look around and *really* didn't like what she saw.

No tower. Now, that was *bad*. Imagine coming home and finding your house gone.

Instead there was an ice house on a sleigh parked under a tree with a large, hulking, angry-looking reindeer idling between the traces. Also bad.

The next bad thing was that the stray dog who always tagged along with Elsie was sitting in the snow, staring at the place where the tower should be and making sad little noises in his throat.

'Well now,' said Magenta aloud. 'What's all *this* about?'

Nuisance looked round, and gave an anxious woof.

'Why ask me where it's gone?' Magenta said to him. '*I* wasn't here.'

She stood for a moment, thinking. If Elsie *had* moved the tower, why hadn't she taken the dog? And *why* had she moved the tower? And *where* was Corbett? And *what* was the weird ice house doing here? Too many questions. Time for some answers.

'Come on, dog,' she said. 'Let's get to the bottom of it, shall we?'

With Nuisance trotting at her heels, Magenta marched over to the ice house. The reindeer lowered its big head and pointed its antlers.

'Don't even think about it, tree head! Stand still or I'll zap you. I've got a wand up my sleeve.'

Spike stood still and watched Magenta hammer loudly on the door.

Now, while the tower has been disappearing and Magenta reappearing, a lot of things have been going on in the ice house too. So let's go back even further to the time when Jack went inside the tower with Elsie and Corbett.

As ordered, Trev and Terry came out to collect the frozen victims of their father's quick temper. Tracy didn't help because she was still sulking in the bathroom.

One by one, Joey, Bill, Sylphine and Nuisance were lugged into the ice house and defrosted.

Trev and Terry knew how to do this – their dad often lost his temper and left them to sort out his mess. Experience taught them to start at the feet, because there was always a row when the mouths got thawed. Joey and Sylphine did indeed have plenty to say, but things calmed down when Trev pointed out that he and his brother were hardly to blame for their dad's finger-happy nature, which was true. Sensibly, nobody suggested tying anyone up. Nuisance wanted to go out and they let him.

It was at this point, outside in the moonlight, that the tower disappeared. But nobody noticed.

Terry made everyone a cup of tea. Apparently, the Frost children actually did Do Hot when their dad wasn't around. Trev suggested a game of Snap, so he, his brother and Joey pulled up ice chairs to the ice table and started dealing out cards.

Tracy, hearing the sound of laughter and feeling

left out, finally came out of the bathroom. With a cry of delight she spotted Sylphine and the girls fell into each other's arms. They both went off to sit on Tracy's ice bed and talk about hair. Card playing not being a wire basket interest, Bill floated off to join them and ended up on Tracy's lap. As it was taking place in an ice house, it wasn't exactly a cosy scene, but it wasn't bad.

All of them gave a jump when they heard the fierce banging.

Trev shovelled the cards into his pocket and Terry went to answer the door.

'Who are you and why are you parked here?' Magenta's voice demanded. 'I see my tower has gone missing. What do you know about that, young man?'

'Magenta!' shouted Joey and Sylphine, leaping to their feet. They crowded in the doorway, along with Bill, who had shot off Tracy's lap.

'You're back!' whooped Joey.

'Where have you been?' squealed Sylphine. 'We've all been so worried.'

'Never mind that,' said Magenta. 'Where's the tower?'

'We don't know,' said Joey. 'Elsie's in there with Jack Frost and—'

'What?' snapped Magenta. 'Jack Frost is *here*?'

'Yes,' said Sylphine. 'He wants to steal the tower and run away in it because he's wanted by the Magic Circle for questioning.'

'I know,' said Magenta. 'We— I mean, the *Circle* has been trying to catch up with him for a while now. We— I mean, *they* thought they had him, which is why we— *they* all assembled to hear what he had to say in his defence and decide what to do, and then he slipped through our— ahem, *their* fingers again.'

'Aha! You're a member of the Magic Circle!' said Joey. 'Maureen said there was a witch representative. It's you! It's okay, we won't say anything.'

'Please don't. What's this house on runners thing and why is it here? Who are these extra people I don't know?'

'This is my friend Tracy,' said Sylphine. 'And these are her brothers, Trev and Terry.'

'Jack's children,' said Joey. 'Well, three of 'em. There are loads more at home.'

'Sorry,' said Trev and Terry hanging their heads. 'About our Dad trying to nick yer place,' went on Trev. 'He's been out of order lately.'

'You can't choose your family,' said Magenta. 'I should know. Look at my sister. Where's Corbett?'

'In the tower with Elsie,' said Joey.

'And where is your fool of a father now?' Magenta asked the boys.

'In the tower, ma'am,' mumbled Trev.

'Tryin' it out to see if it suits,' muttered Terry.

'Sorry,' they both chorused.

'He'll be the one who's sorry when the Magic

Circle catches up with him. What will you three do then?'

'Go back to Ma's,' said Terry. 'Have a hot meal.'

'Stay out of trouble,' said his brother.

'Ask Ma if I can have a sleepover at Sylphine's,' said Tracy. 'She's my best friend.'

At this point – as if there wasn't already a lot going on – the tower reappeared in the clearing! The door opened and Elsie jumped out. Corbett flew behind her. He spotted Magenta immediately, let out a happy squawk, and flapped wildly to her shoulder.

'Ouch,' said Magenta. 'Mind the claws, annoying bird!!'

'I won't say I've missed you,' said Corbett, 'but it's good to have you back.'

Elsie ran into the arms of Joey and Sylphine

and the three of them danced around, Nuisance barking at their heels and Bill doing happy roll-overs in the air.

It was a great reunion, with everyone talking over each other, trying to explain what had been happening.

There were, of course, many gaps to be filled. Magenta wanted to know everything that had occurred while she was gone. Everyone wanted to know what had kept her away for so long. Now that the secret was out about her being a witch representative on the Magic Circle, there was no point in her keeping things from the others. Apparently, an emergency meeting had been called to decide what to do about Jack Frost, who had been running around freezing forests, towns and villages and trapping them in endless winters. As most meetings do, it took

much longer than she thought, but at least the hotel she was staying at had good room service.

'I wrote and told you to get Elsie to cover for me until I got back,' she said to Corbett.

'Never arrived. It was snowing. There was no post and I couldn't get to her for five days.'

'Well, that was hardly my fault, was it? And I wasn't to know that Jack Frost had the cheek to come snooping around in the hopes of getting his hands on my tower.'

'It's not *my* fault either if you don't have the common courtesy to leave me a note in the first place.'

And so it went on. It was good to see them back on the same comfortable bad terms.

Magenta was delighted to hear that Elsie kept her head and managed to strand Jack Frost on a tropical island. She would go and inform the Magic Circle, who would send someone to pick him up and bring him in for long overdue questioning.

'Elsie,' she said, 'you did well. I think you can call yourself a fully-fledged witch now.'

Magenta didn't often give away compliments. Elsie glowed with happiness.

After all the explanations, there was a celebration cake, provided by the magic larder. Then there were goodbyes, as Spike took the three Frosts back to their ma. Sylphine actually wept as the ice sledge pulled away. Nobody asked whether her tears were for Tracy or Spike.

And that brings us back to the three children and Corbett, sitting and chatting at the kitchen table, eating pancakes, watching the snow melt and Spring arrive. Magenta was upstairs having a lie-in.

After breakfast, Elsie walked home with Nuisance. It was time she went back to Smallbridge. Now that the snow was gone, the Emporium would open again and her dad would need her help.

She hoped there would be more adventures to come. More magic. More excitement. More fun. After all, she was a fully-fledged witch now.

But all that lay ahead. There was no rush. Right now, she was strolling through the forest, eating a chocolate egg with Nuisance at her side.

She would just stop and pick a bunch of early Spring primroses . . .

Acknowledgements

The terrific team at Simon and Schuster, especially my lovely editor, Jane. Ashley, my talented illustrator, who has brought Elsie's world to life. My good friend and fantastic literary agent, Caroline Sheldon. My always supportive husband Mo and daughter Ella. All my loyal readers, young and not so young. All the bookshops and libraries who buy this book. The cats who let me cuddle them whenever I get stuck.

Follow Elsie in her other adventures

KAYE UMANSKY

Witch for a Week

'Certain to delight any witch in the making'
M.G. LEONARD

Illustrated by
ASHLEY KING